LISTEN. WHILE THE memory lasts, listen to the adventures of a man. A man? Is that all?

Yes, a man. Not a giant, nor one of the Immortals. Just a man. He had a wife, a son, a dog, and a boat. And though he was a king, his kingdom was small and rocky and hemmed in by the disrespectful sea.

No, Odysseus was not a giant or an Immortal. But when he fought in the Trojan War he won the name of hero. And as he traveled home from the War, he met with such adventures that the gods themselves looked down with bated breath. The gods helped him and the gods hindered him. And the gods squabbled as they watched Odysseus struggle across the face of the world-encircled sea.

From his castle in Ithaca, his queen, Penelope, looked out and saw only sea. Day after day she watched for Odysseus in his brightly painted boat. But he did not come and he did not come and he did not ever come. . . .

Odysseus

RETOLD BY
Geraldine
McCaughrean

Cricket Books/Chicago

HEROES

Text copyright © 2003 by Geraldine McCaughrean
Illustration copyright © 2004 by Tom Kidd
All rights reserved
Printed in the United States of America
Interior designed by Gina M. Kelsey

Eighth Printing 2014

Library of Congress Cataloging-in-Publication Data

McCaughrean, Geraldine.
    Odysseus / Geraldine McCaughrean.— 1st American ed.
        p. cm. — (Heroes)
    ISBN 0-8126-2721-0
    1. Odysseus (Greek mythology)—Juvenile literature. 2. Mythology, Greek—Juvenile literature. I. Title.
    BL820.O3M37 2004
    398.2′0938′02—dc22

                                2004010734

The Maple Press Manufacturing Group
York, PA, USA

February 2014

Eighth printing

For Abi

Contents

The Mighty Monsters and Immortals in *Odysseus*

AEOLUS—Keeper of the Winds

ATHENE—Goddess of War and Wisdom

CALYPSO—nymph who keeps Odysseus on her island for seven years

CERBERUS—monstrous three-headed dog that guards the entrance to the Underworld

CHARYBDIS—sea monster in the form of a raging whirlpool

CIRCE—powerful goddess/sorceress who turns Odysseus's men into pigs

HELIOS—Sun God

HERMES—Messenger of the Gods

LAESTRYGONIANS—giant cannibals

PLUTO—God of the Underworld (also known as Hades)

POLYPHEMUS—Cyclops, son of Poseidon

POSEIDON—God of the Sea and Earthquakes

SCYLLA—six-headed sea monster that lives in a cave opposite from Charybdis and snatches sailors from their ships and devours them

SIRENS—sea nymphs who lure sailors to their island and certain death by singing to them

ZEUS—Ruler of the Gods

The Family of Odysseus*

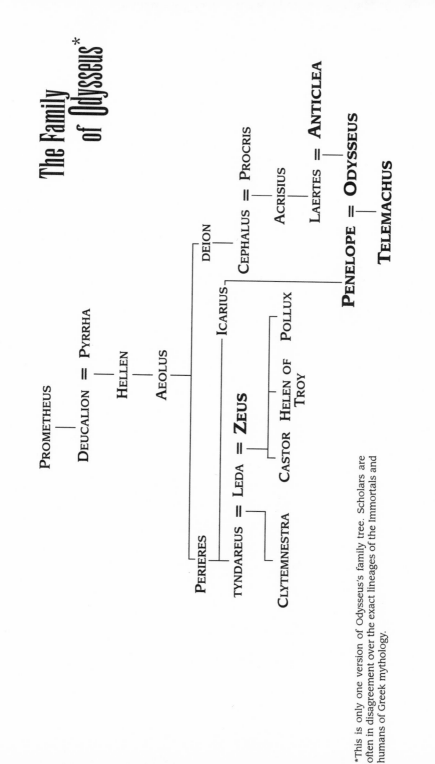

*This is only one version of Odysseus's family tree. Scholars are often in disagreement over the exact lineages of the Immortals and humans of Greek mythology.

Chapter One

The Land of the Lotus Eaters

"WHEN WILL FATHER come home?"

Queen Penelope turned away from the bright window to look at her son. "Soon, Telemachus. Soon."

"But the war has been over a long time now," said the boy, fingering his father's golden spear and quiver of polished satinwood.

"Troy is a long way away—the other side of the world-encircled sea, on the far eastern shore. If there are no winds in his favor, his men can only row. It would take many, many months to row from Troy to Ithaca."

Telemachus tried to lift the huge sword that stood in the corner of the room, but it was too heavy for him. How much more must the king's sword of gold weigh that his father had worn when he went away to war!

"Why don't I remember his face, Mother?"

"Child! You were only a baby when he sailed for Troy. The siege lasted for ten years. I can describe him to you—how his hair curls forward from the crown, how he wears his beard trimmed to a point, how his tan is darker than the mainland Greeks', who never sail between the sun and the sea. And his hair is almost the color of his bronze helmet—ah, I forget, you never saw his warrior's helmet, or his blue eyes looking out. I can describe him to you, child, but I wish there were someone to describe his son to him . . . or that he were here to see you for himself."

"But you say he'll come soon, Mother?" said Telemachus.

"As soon as the gods allow. This island of ours, this Ithaca, it's his home. It's his kingdom. And what use is a king without a kingdom or a kingdom without a king?"

And her eyes returned to the sea below the palace, to the brimming ocean, whose waves were always arriving, always beaching, on Ithaca's rocky shore.

In the prow of his boat, Odysseus stood and gazed ahead at the gray swell of the sea, which seemed always to be moving but never arriving. And he longed for the rocky shores of Ithaca and for his dear wife, Penelope, and for a sight of the son he had seen only as a baby.

For ten days the wind had torn white spume off the wavetops. It scudded into the clouds and mixed sky with sea so that there was no horizon. Odysseus's twelve ships had been driven aslant across the heaving water, and his sailors had lifted their oars for fear they'd be smashed like twigs. Not even the seamanship of their captain could steer them where they wanted to go or tell them where the storm had brought them.

Somehow the twelve boats had stayed together.

Somehow none had been snatched down by the sea. And now they were sailing in unknown waters, and the exhausted men lay slumped over their oars. The twelve sails hung in strips, slit from top to bottom three, four times. And Odysseus was at the prow of his ship watching for some friendly sign of land.

There! A cluster of birds, rising like ash from a bonfire, hung in the sky over a yellow coastline.

"Look and praise the gods! There's rest and food and fresh water for you. Lean on your oars and let the first crew ashore be the first to go foraging!"

In each ship the oars rattled home between their thole-pins, and forty-four wooden blades sliced white slits in the creamy ocean. The lead ship moved forward with such a leap that the cockerel on the stern—Odysseus's own mascot—was unbalanced and spread its speckled wings and threw back its scarlet comb and crowed with all its might.

The shores of the island were turquoise where the sea spread transparent skirts over soft, white sand. The ships slipped ashore with such ease that the weary sailors could simply step over the sides and throw themselves down on the warm, white dunes beneath the shade of palm trees. Most fell asleep then and there. But the first crew to step ashore was eager to press inland to find what lay beyond a green clump of palms.

"Be careful," said Odysseus. "Find out what people or beasts live here. They may be unfriendly. They may be

3

frightened by five hundred strangers on their shores. Tread carefully."

So the foraging party agreed to take care and to return by nightfall with news of the land's people and animals and plants. On the beach, Odysseus lay down and waited.

As the sun went down, and the low light poured thick as honey through the sea lanes and dry-land pathways, he watched for his crew to return. Night fell over land and sea alike, and a million stars cascaded. But the crew of the first ship did not come and did not come and did not ever come.

"Do you think they've been ambushed, lord?" asked Polites, captain of the tenth ship. "Or maybe wild animals have eaten them or trapped them somewhere in the darkness."

"Bring your crew, and we'll go and see. But let us be stealthy. Remember how we had to fight the Cicones in Thrace when they had us outnumbered. I don't want to lose more good men in fighting."

So without helmets or swords to clatter, the second party crept off the beach and inshore, through thickly and more thickly wooded pathways. They could hear the pretty tinkling of fresh water. In the darkness, they could smell the thick, sweet smell of coconut. And as they felt their way, the plush skins of hanging fruit brushed their hands and faces, and over-arching blossoms dropped petals in their hair.

All at once, dawn stood in the sky and let fall strands of golden light, like curls of hair. Odysseus and his company found themselves on the edge of a beautiful clearing, where a glistening pool lay full of early morning sunlight.

Stretched out on its shores, in their dark and gleaming skin, lay smiling men and women. And in among them—their sword belts unfastened and their helmets full of fruit—sprawled the crew of the first boat. Raucous laughter flew back and forth across the pool, and the light flashed on the rims of bronze bowls piled high with succulent fruit. A girl was picking still more from the overhanging trees. So soft and ripe it was, that the juice ran down her arms. She carried it to the sprawling Greeks who crammed it into their mouths and threw the stones—*plop*—into the center of the pool.

In his hiding place, Odysseus was speechless with amazement. But Polites leaped forward into the clearing and called out angrily, "Why didn't you come and tell us about all this? Did you want to keep it all to yourselves?"

The idle soldiers grinned and waved their hands. The dark-skinned strangers smiled, too, and hurried to bring a bowl of fruit to the newcomers. But Odysseus (who was quick of hand, but quicker still of wit) took the bowl and held it in the crook of his arm, untasted. "Stir yourselves, men! We've got a long day's rowing ahead of us."

A disheveled soldier flapped one hand at Odysseus. "What? Leave our friends here? For what? To heave some wooden hulk over the lousy sea? Sit down, why don't you? Have some fruit. By all the gods on Olympus, it's the most delicious stuff you ever ate in your life!"

The soldiers behind Odysseus were anxious to taste the wonderful fruit and jostled forward. But Odysseus held up his hand and continued speaking in a loud, good-humored voice. "Not as good as your wife's goat stew, surely, Stavros—and nothing to compare with the first cup of cold wine your daughter will bring you as you beach on the shores of Ithaca?"

The soldier picked up another fruit and bit into it and let the juice run down his chin and chest before answering. "Ten years we've been gone from Ithaca. My wife will be old and fat by now. My daughter—she'll be married and good riddance. This is the life for me."

The man next to him sniggered and scratched his head. "I'm beggared if I can remember if I'm married or not. Seems to me I did have a wife once. Ach, who needs one? I'll live on fruit and friendship till I die!"

Polites and Odysseus exchanged glances. "I know that man," said Polites under his breath. "He has nine children waiting for him at home. What spell have these devils put on him?"

Odysseus showed the bowl by way of reply. "Have you seen what they're eating? The fruit of the lotus tree. By tomorrow they won't remember Ithaca itself, let alone their wives and children. Tell your men, and warn them on no account to taste the fruit. When I give the word, let two good men each seize on one poor fool and carry him back to the boat. Something tells me it won't be easy, either. I've heard tell of these Lotus Eaters."

The dark-skinned strangers were pressing close round Odysseus now, with smiles and outstretched hands, full of fruit. "Rest! Eat! You're welcome to everything we have!" they seemed to say. But Odysseus slipped free of their juice-sticky hands and, with a shout, seized on Stavros and flung him over his shoulder. His soldiers fell on their companions—two to one—and hauled them to their feet, belaboring them with reproaches: "Think of your wife! Think of your children! Think of Ithaca!"

But the lotus-eating Greeks only clung to their precious fruit and cursed and struggled. As they were overpowered, they begged to be allowed to stay. They implored Odysseus to leave them, forget them. Then they began to cry and sob pitifully. Stavros beat with his fists on Odysseus's broad back and howled, "Please don't make me go! This is my home! This is where I belong! Don't make me leave my friends. The fruit! At least take some fruit aboard! I'll die if I don't have more fruit!"

Closing their ears to the wailing, Odysseus and Polites led the way back to the beach, calling ahead for the boats to be made ready. The juice-sticky natives followed on for a time, clinging to their Greeks, wheedling and pleading and all the time smiling. But they would not be parted long from their beloved trees and began

7

to drop off like contented leeches and patter back toward the clearing.

On the shore, five hundred men sprang to their feet. Masts were lifted, rooted in the deep sockets of the boats' keels. Sails were raised. Oars were run out.

"Put them aboard and lash them under the thwarts!" commanded Odysseus. And the writhing and wriggling Lotus Eaters were stuffed under the seats like so many furled sails and bound there with strong rope. The dismayed crews heaved their boats off the soft, clinging sand and into the surf, then leaped aboard and leaned on their oars. And in every boat, forty wooden blades sliced white slits in the creamy ocean. The lead ship moved forward with such a leap that the cockerel on the stern unbalanced and spread its speckled wings and threw back its scarlet comb and crowed triumphantly.

Chapter Two

Polyphemus and the Man Called No Wun

ALL AT ONCE, dawn stood in the sky and let fall strands of golden light, like curls of hair. Odysseus's fleet lay on the open sea. The gentle water was dinted like hammered gold, and rowing was easy. In time, the madness of the Lotus Eaters died in their hollow stomachs, and they took their places, shamefaced, at their empty oars.

At the stern of every boat, great amphoras of blood-red wine were rammed into heaps of sand, to keep them upright. Odysseus had looted the wine from the Cicones in Thrace, and though the enterprise had cost him six good men out of every boat, they now had wine enough for the journey, however long it proved. The wine was so strong that they drank it diluted ten times over with water, for fear of falling insensible over their oars. No, drink was not lacking, even when the sun hammered day after day on the dinted golden sea. But there was not a morsel of food in the boats. They had to find land and sustenance quickly.

There! A spire of dust and a choir of bleats hung in the air over a craggy, wooded island. As the boats drew closer, the men could see shaggy, long-horned goats watching them from every ledge of the cliff-ringed shore.

In each ship, the oars rattled between the thole-pins, and forty-four wooden blades sliced white slits in the brazen ocean. Odysseus stood at the prow with his cockerel on his arm, and, as the ship leaped forward, the cock's talons sank in and drew blood as red as the comb on its head. It gave a squawk that chilled the sweat of those that heard it—even under the brazen sun.

The little island was uninhabited except for the goats. But from the top of its single pointed hill, Odysseus could see across a strait to fertile land. Terraces of vines and olive trees plumed gray-green above the shore, and there was a harbor guarded by elegant, swaying, black poplars, like Trojan sentries in their plumed helmets.

"This time I shall go and reconnoiter, myself," said Odysseus. "Eleven ships will stay here. I and my men will go across the strait to scout about."

On the far shore, Odysseus chose just twelve of his best men to venture farther inland. All they carried with them for baggage was an amphora of wine to offer as a gift to the king of the country. At the very top of the slopes, huge arching cave mouths embellished with vines showed that men lived here. But Odysseus did not have to climb so far before finding a cave with a walled yard in front of it, ripe with the smell of sheep. No one was inside.

"Look, Captain! Cheeses! And look at the size of them!" cried a soldier, trying to lift a cheese as big as a millstone. "Let's take these before the owner comes back. They'll last us all the way to Ithaca!"

"Where's the hurry?" said Odysseus. "I've a mind to see what kind of a man builds walls this high and makes cheeses like these. The laws of hospitality will oblige him to give us food and presents. We might get better than cheese to take away with us! And since when did Greek fighting men have anything to fear from a shepherd?"

So the scouting party went inside the cave and settled themselves down to wait for the shepherd's return.

The sun sank down, and the low light poured thick as honey through the olive grove, vineyards, and the mouth of the cave. All round the cave walls, between the heaps of dung, pans of milk were settling into curds and whey. From the size of the pans, the skimming spoon, the firewood, and a great club lying on the floor, Odysseus knew that the owner must be a giant of extraordinary strength. But nothing prepared him for the creature that came.

A herd of sheep and goats, huge as cows and horses, clattered down the slope and into the yard. Behind them came a hill—an overgrown hillock of sinews and rolling flesh. Hairy skin, with pores as big as rabbit holes, wrinkled over the muscle and bone of a breathing, walking mountain. Odysseus might have called it a man, but for the one giant eye that stood in its hideous forehead, above the cavernous nostrils and the pothole of a mouth.

The moment the ogre had chased the last of his animals inside, he rolled across the gateway a boulder so huge that twenty Greeks could not have rolled it away again. Then he kindled a fire, and yellow light washed over the floor and up the walls of rock.

"Well, well, well. And who have we here?" said the one-eyed giant.

"Ha-ha. A dozen poor, unfortunate Greeks sheltering from weariness and hunger in the hospitable portals of your charming home," said Odysseus, walking forward jauntily and greeting the ogre with a wave of his hand. "Ha-ha. We might have been scared out of our skins by your . . . your ample size. But we are the servants of Great Zeus, father of all the gods, and of course we know that no god-fearing man would do harm to a fellow servant of Zeus."

The ogre squatted down with his hands spread over his grinning mouth and peered at Odysseus with his one great rheumy eye. "Is that so? Is that so? Well, and surely you aren't all alone on the big ocean? Just the . . . eight . . . ten . . . thirteen of you? Are there no more? Where's your boat, good sir?"

But Odysseus (who was quick of hand, but quicker still of wit) said, "Brother! I'm appalled to have to tell you that our boat was wrecked on that promontory beyond

the beach—smashed to pieces. We are the only sur-
vivors. Still, we count ourselves fortunate to have found
our way here to your delightful home. May I have the
honor of knowing your name?"

The ogre's mouth gaped in a laugh as noisy as falling
trees. He reached over Odysseus's head, picked up two
of his crew—the fattest ones—and smashed them heads-
down on the floor. He ate them then like men eat slivers
of honeycomb trying not to lose a drop of the juice. And
he said, while his mouth was still full, "So, you think
Polyphemus ought to be frightened of old Zeus, do you?
Huh! You ignorant little worm. Why should a Cyclops
give a spit what Zeus thinks? Least of all Polyphemus,
son of the great god Poseidon, who just now smashed
your boat like an eggshell. My father stands in the ocean
trench and chews on the clouds. Poseidon has the better
of Zeus, as Polyphemus has the better of . . . what did
you say your name was?"

Most of the crew were huddled together against the
back of the cave, weeping at the terrible death of their
friends. But Odysseus said, "I didn't tell you my name.
And why should I tell it to an unholy monster like you? I
shall keep it secret now, till I die!"

"Oh, don't be like that! You're my guest! Tell me your
name. Go on. Tell me. I'll grant you a favor if you tell me."

"Oh, very well, then," said Odysseus. "My name is No
Wun. Now spare the rest of us if only because we are
your guests!"

13

Polyphemus picked his teeth. "No Wun. What a stupid name. All right, No Wun. Because you're my guests, I promise I won't eat another man . . . until breakfast time! Ha-ha-ha!"

Delighted with this joke of his, the hideous Cyclops lay down beside the fire and went to sleep on his back so that he snored all night long.

At the sound of the first snore, Odysseus's men drew their swords, ready to stab the creature in its knotty neck. But Odysseus held up his hand and whispered urgently, "Don't be so rash! If we managed to kill him, how would we shift the boulder out of the doorway? We'd be trapped in here like prawns in a pot until the other giants came looking. A mouth for every man of us, I dare say."

"What then, Lord Odysseus?" said the youngest man of all, trying to hide his helpless tears. "The goddess Athene made you quick of hand and even quicker of wit, so save us from being eaten!"

Odysseus was looking at the giant club or shepherd's crook that lay in one corner of the cave. "There might be a way," he said. "For all but four of us."

At dawn the Cyclops grunted and opened his one bleary eye. Quickly Odysseus kicked dung over the crook. All night long they had sat blunting their swords on it, hacking off splinters of the hard wood. As Odysseus nonchalantly scuffed dung over the hiding place, his men embraced each other for fear Polyphemus had wakened hungry.

14

None too soon did they say their good-byes. The Cyclops reached out one lazy hand and then another, and chose two thick-set men for his breakfast. He bit into them like apples and spat out their belts like pips. Then rolling back the stone in the door and shooing out his sheep and goats, he fixed his malicious eye on the Greeks. "Until tonight, honored guests," he said, grinning. And ducking outside, he rolled the stone back across the mouth of their prison. The sound of the bells round the animals' necks grew more and more distant.

Horror and misery paralyzed the poor, trapped men. They looked into each other's faces and wondered, "Will it be you or will it be me for supper?" All day long, as they faced each other across the massive shepherd's crook and hacked at it with their blades, they wondered, "Will it be you or will it be me?" Sooner than they wanted, they had their answer.

Polyphemus unsealed the cave and drove in his goats and sheep. There was no chance of a dash to freedom before the stone was in place again. Choosing two of the crew, Polyphemus nibbled them like skewered lamb, then crunched on their bones for the marrow.

"I brought you a present—before I knew you for what you are," said Odysseus as the Cyclops wiped his mouth on his forearm. "It would have gone down well, too, with that miserable meal of yours."

"Oh, give it to me, No Wun! I like presents! I'll tell you what: give me my present, and I'll grant you all the honor due to a guest of mine. Is it a bargain?"

15

"A bargain," said Odysseus. He and two others crawled into the darkest recess of the cave and fetched the amphora of wine. Polyphemus's one bulging eye gleamed. He grabbed the great stone jar, lifting it without the least strain, and drank a greedy swig.

"No Wun, this is delicious! Nectar! A drop of liquid sunlight. I have vines of my own, but my wine tastes like . . . vigenar compared with . . . like nivegar . . . like givenar . . . oof! This stuff is strong, No Wun!"

"Before you drink it all, you owe me a favor," said Odysseus tartly.

"Thasstrue. Very droo! How troo-oo-oo!" slurred the ogre, wagging one drunken finger. "Tell you whassit to be! I'll eat you la-la-lasht! Ha-ha-ha!"

Overjoyed with this joke of his and hiccupping happily, he keeled over onto his back and fell asleep beside the fire.

Throwing aside the clods of dung, the Greeks unearthed the crook they had sharpened to a point with their swords. This point they hardened in the hot embers of the fire until it glowed red hot and was on the verge of bursting into flames. Humping it onto their shoulders, they ran at the Cyclops's lolling head, lifted the wooden shaft and plunged it into his one, closed, flickering eye—right through the lid.

The scream deafened them, like the clap of a bell deafens a man with his head inside it. They scattered to all corners of the cave, holding their hands over their ears to dull the re-echoing, redoubling roar. Frightened sheep lumbered up against them. Polyphemus's hands groped for them . . . and the rest of the night lay ahead.

Giants from the caves higher up the hill heard the agony of Polyphemus and were roused from their beds. Their gigantic feet could be heard displacing rocks as they slithered down the steep paths in the darkness. "What's the matter, Polyphemus? What's the matter?"

"My eye! My eye! I'm blinded!" screamed Polyphemus from inside his cave. "Help me!"

"Who did it, Polyphemus? Who has done this terrible thing to you?" they shouted back.

"No Wun! No Wun did it! No Wun blinded me!"

There were grunts and disgruntled noises from the outer darkness. "An accident, maybe," said one voice.

"Struck blind by the gods, maybe," said another.

"In that case, his father can help him. Let's not cross the gods by interfering."

"Too dark for dressing wounds, anyway," said a voice growing smaller as the speaker climbed back up the hill.

All night stars cascaded in the sky. But Odysseus and his men, sealed in the cave, did not see them, and Polyphemus would never see them again. He groped and scrabbled about for the Greeks, but felt only his animals and their udders fat with milk. When morning came, the animals wanted to be out in the sun, with grass and leaves to eat.

Still groaning and grinding his teeth with agony, the

giant Cyclops crawled to the boulder blocking the entry. He rolled it away, but immediately sat down across the doorway, with his hands barring the gap to either side of his hips.

"Try it! Just try to escape!" he taunted his prisoners. "I'll swat you like flies and eat you slowly, slowly, slowly." The goats stumbled forward and he fumbled furious fingers over each one before letting it pass by and run free.

Odysseus was too busy to tremble. He was dragging together the giant sheep and lashing them, three by three, side by side, with rushes from the matting on the floor. Beneath each middle sheep, a member of his crew clung to handfuls of fleece. The sheep bleated forward toward the doorway, and Polyphemus fumbled furious fingers over each back, side, head, and tail. But of course he could not feel the man slung beneath each center sheep. Soon only Odysseus remained and only one sheep. It was the biggest animal of all—a ram with coiled horns and clumps of fleece that overhung it like snow over-hangs a mountaintop.

Odysseus crawled underneath the ram and clung so tightly to its fleece that his arms and legs were smothered in wool. The big ram headed for the daylight, which crept in round the giant shape of the Cyclops. Polyphemus stopped it with his right hand.

"What's this, Woolly? Are you last of all, today?" said the ogre, recognizing his ram by its coiled horns and wealth of wool. "You're usually first away, first out to eat the green grass. Oh, Woolly! I'll never see it again, that green grass! I'm blind! Blind, Woolly! Blackness. Nothing but blackness between now and forever. Dear, handsome Woolly, how will I see to pick the burrs out of your fleece, now? Oh! If you could just speak! Just for a moment! You could tell me where they were hiding. You could direct me to those repulsive little Greek ticks so I could stamp on them one by one. You'd do that for me, wouldn't you, old friend? If you just had the wits and the words. Go on with you. Go on. Leave me in my blackness. But come back soon tonight. After I've killed the Greek lice, I'll be lonely here in the darkness."

The great woolly ram trotted off, slowly because of the weight of Odysseus hanging in its fleece. Not until he was a sunray's breadth from the cave did Odysseus let himself drop and lie on the stony ground, enjoying the sight of the blue sky.

His men mustered round him. They ran helter-skelter down the goat paths to their solitary boat, and their six paltry oars sliced six white slits in the ocean. But under the quarter-deck and thwarts were lashed a dozen giant sheep for their meat.

To reach the island where the other ships were waiting, they had to sail right below Polyphemus's high-arching cave. From its perch on the stern, Odysseus's cockerel crowed into the face of the sun, an arrogant, piercing crow. They saw the ogre cock his head and turn toward the sea, his one empty eye socket staring. Pride welled up in Odysseus, and he, too, crowed like the cockerel: "Hey! You with the blind eye! Do you see what comes of scorning Zeus? Great Zeus and the goddess Athene—she of the two beautiful, gray, and shining eyes—sent us to teach you humility! So much for the son of Poseidon!"

Polyphemus gave a bellow of anguish and knelt up, his frame casting a shadow over the whole length of the boat. He picked up the boulder from the doorway of the cave and hurled it in the direction of Odysseus's voice.

It fell just ahead of the prow, and a huge wave pitched the boat backward for twice its length—almost smashing it against the shore. The crew only saved it by heaving on the oars with all their might.

Odysseus laughed crowingly and wagged his fists in the air. "Missed, Polyphemus! Don't you wish you had your eye now?"

"Sit down, Captain! Sit down, please!" his men begged him. "One more boulder like that and we are dead men, for all your cunning and wit!"

But the cruelty of battle welled up in Odysseus, such as he had not felt since he saw Troy burn. He cupped his hands round his mouth and yelled, "Know this, Polyphemus! That it was Odysseus, King of Ithaca, who blinded you and stole your woolly sheep. That is my true name, and darkness is your true fate forever and a day!"

This time Polyphemus did not let out a shout. He rose silently to his feet and stretched out both arms toward the sky he could not see. "Poseidon! Hear me! Father and god who stands in the ocean trench and chews on the black storm clouds—look down from holy Olympus and see what Odysseus of Ithaca has done to your only son! Blind! Blind as night, I am, forever and a day. Reach up out of the sea! Reach down out of the clouds! And plunge him and all his boats deeper than the depth where all fishes are blind. Forbid that he should ever see wife or home again, since I shall see no such comfort! And let his doom be remembered on every shore that fringes the world-encircled sea!"

His swinging fists smashed a gobbet of rock out of the cliff face, and, raising it over his head, he hurled it down on the sound of the ship's dipping oars.

It fell just behind the stern, and a huge wave picked up the boat and flung it, spinning on the crest, across the narrow straits, and drove it ashore on the beach of the desolate, uninhabited island. Startled goats scattered. But for a time no man moved from the oar he was grasping. For a time, no man breathed.

"Take out that huge ram of mine and roast it here on the beach! And let's offer it up to Zeus for our happy escape!" cried Odysseus.

The six remaining men looked up at him across their oars, and the sheep bleated under the thwarts. After a time, they did as he said, according to every rule of holy law. Afterward they and the crews of the other boats roasted other sheep and greatly enjoyed eating them, washed down with Ciconian wine.

But they did not omit to plant each of the six empty oars upright on the shore and to call the names of their oarsmen three times across the mist-smothered sea, so that they might always be remembered.

Night fell over land and sea lanes alike, and a million stars cascaded. From the top of a lonely summit, Odysseus looked up at them and saw huge navy clouds swell like pride and blot out the stars one by one. At last only one bright star remained, awash in the night sky, like a shipwrecked sailor afloat in the world-encircled sea. The waves breaking on the shore of the little island seemed to whisper, "Poseidon. Poseidon. Poseidon."

Chapter Three

A Parcel of Wind

WITH THEIR HOLDS filled with fresh meat and their amphoras with good wine, enough for any journey, the men of Ithaca rowed on across the brimming sea. Like slices of lemon, they bobbed in the bowl of shining water where the gods dip their hands. And sail and tide and rowing brought them to an unmapped island.

There! A blinding flash of light signaled the sun's reflection off some shining shore. But the island that came into view had no chalk cliffs, no sand dunes, no scrubby green hills. It was encircled by a shining wall of golden bronze—without steps, without rungs, without even the heads of nails to give a man footholds to climb up. And as the ocean nudged it, the whole vast island rocked and yawed. It had no roots of bronze sunk in the ocean bed and no anchor to hold it in place. The island of Aeolia drifted wherever wind and the tides carried it.

As the bulwarks of the twelve boats banged gently against the bronze, and the men laughed at the sight of their own reflections and combed their matted beards,

Odysseus stood up in the prow and hailed the inhabitants of this colossal fort. He had no sooner started to speak than a basket, secured with four strong ropes, was lowered down. It was large enough for only one man, and, without hesitation, Odysseus himself leaped in. "Hold off your boats until I return," he called. "There may be presents for everyone from such a handsome realm."

Odysseus was not disappointed. He was helped from the basket and escorted most courteously to the dining hall of King Aeolus. There seemed to be a feast in progress, for a long table was laid with bronze, silver, and golden dishes, with places enough for six on each side and for Aeolus and his queen at either end.

At the mention of Odysseus's name, the king knew at once what voyage the twelve ships were on. "In drifting here and there, we have met with many a Greek ship homeward bound from Troy. And every storyteller aboard every ship had some heroic story to tell about Odysseus. They say the gray-eyed Athene gave you cunning hands and still more cunning wit. But why so long voyaging? Aren't you heading a long way round for your beloved island of Ithaca?"

Odysseus thanked the king for his gracious compliments and explained about the storms that had blown for ten days and beaten the fleet to the southernmost shore of the sea-encircling world.

"Ah! I recollect that storm! Poseidon, the Earth-Shaker, the Sea-Breaker, was restless and quarrelsome.

Why do you flinch like that at the name of Poseidon? You have nothing to fear from him. Why, at present there's not a banner of wind flying over the ocean that I didn't hoist myself. Zeus entrusted the winds to me—as a lesson to old Poseidon for his surly bad temper. After our meal I'll show them to you. Now, fetch another chair and set another place for the heroic Odysseus, terror of the Trojans!"

Tempted as he was, Odysseus was unwilling to eat while his men went hungry down below. But King Aeolus saw what was in his mind and said, "As much as we eat here I shall command to be lowered down to your ships. No honest servant of the gods ever comes to Aeolia and goes away unsatisfied."

Just then the king's family entered to the sound of music. Six handsome sons and six radiant daughters, all with hair the color of bronze, took their places at table. And when Odysseus spoke of his travels, they listened as attentively as only islanders can, valuing the news of travelers.

Indeed, Odysseus thought that loneliness must be worse for men on Aeolia than for any man on his own islands of Ithaca, Cephalonia, or little wooded Zanthe, for there were so few of them. Aeolus and his family, with their few trusted servants, alone peopled the huge, bronze-fendered realm. From the white elmwood of the hall's ceiling hung clusters of delicate shells, and as the family talked, their breath and laughter set the shells tinkling with a sound like the laughter of the gods themselves. Night fell outside, and a million stars cascaded, but not with a sweeter music than the tinkling of the Aeolian air.

"If your sons ever travel across the glossy ocean's back, they must come to Ithaca and stay at my palace and enjoy what food and gifts I have to share with them," said Odysseus. "I'm sure they could not lay eyes on the maidens of Ithaca without choosing them for wives."

King Aeolus seemed confused, his sons and daughters embarrassed. "But we never leave this realm or travel, except where Aeolia takes us. Here we have everything we need: for each daughter a husband, for each son a wife, and for me as fine a queen as Penelope of Ithaca must seem in the eyes of Odysseus. You see, I married my sons to my daughters, my daughters to my sons. Now they need never step one pace away from Aeolia: everything they need is here."

The lord Odysseus blushed at his mistake and turned the conversation to stories of battle and heroic deeds, forged in the heat of Troy.

All at once, dawn stood in the sky and let fall light like curls of golden hair. They had feasted the night away, and Aeolus had served every manner of delicacy, sending the same to the boats below.

Odysseus rose to take his leave, but it seemed there was to be one last present more magnificent than the rest. As Aeolus clapped his hands, four strong servants carried in a massive, cowhide bag. The drawstring round its neck was plaited out of strands of silver wire and white silk and, as it stood on the floor, some of its folds unfolded, the creases creased and recreased.

"In this bag are all the winds but one. I've left free only the wind from the south-east, to sit in your sails as far as Ithaca. Your men can ship their oars and sleep. No one but the man at the tiller is needed. You'll be home in a matter of days."

"Of all the presents any man ever gave me, none was more welcome than this," said Odysseus, embracing the cheerful king. "But how can I return them? Surely Zeus entrusted the winds to you? He'll look to you for their safekeeping."

"As soon as you're safely home, loose the cord and set free the other winds. Be careful how you do it, or you may raise a hurricane! The winds will scatter and blow this way and that. But I and my sons can gather them up again as we float about the oceans. Now, be on your way, or that son of yours will be a grown man before you ever see him!"

A shiver shook Odysseus, though no draft set the strung shells tinkling overhead. Delight soon took its place, however, as he watched the servants of King Aeolus hoist the great bag over the bronze parapet and lower it down into his boat.

When Odysseus himself was lowered down, he found his men asleep in the bilges, asleep along the thwarts, asleep over their oars. The twelve boats bobbed against the bronze wall, chipping their bright paintwork, and the captain's noble cockerel was pecking on the dregs of the feast. A lively south-easterly breeze had already sprung up and was going to waste, with no sails to catch it. "Stir yourselves, men! Look to your sails! Draw in your oars and prepare yourselves for your wives' nagging. I myself shall take the tiller. The wind's in our favor, and Ithaca is waiting!"

In each ship, the oars rattled inboard from between their thole-pins, and twelve mended and tattered sails flowered against their mast-stems. They filled with wind, and the fleet leaped forward—so fast that the cockerel perched on the stern made angry noises in its throat.

So Odysseus stood on the quarter-deck, his arm on the tiller and the great cowhide bag stowed beneath. He rested one foot on the knot of the silver cord. He was so eager for the first sight of Ithaca—its craggy green hills, its stony terraces of corn, the tall Mount Neriton rising from its heart—that he could not rest his back or close his eyes or lay down his head and sleep. For ten long days and nights he eased on the tiller, swung on the tiller, leaned on the tiller, and blessed King Aeolus and the great god Zeus for the lively south-east wind.

There! There were the green nodding heads of the trees on little Zanthe. And there beyond was the great black scowling brow of Cephalonia. "If I close my eyes for a moment, then open them again, I shall see my beloved Ithaca. Easy to stay awake with the hope of my own bed to sleep in tonight. Easy to stay awake . . . even if I close my eyes. . . . "

But when he rested his head on his arm, his arm on the tiller, and his back against the stern, he was soon sound asleep, his foot sliding down off the bag's silver cord.

"Thought he'd never sleep," said Eurylochus to the man alongside him. "What is he guarding so carefully in that bag? It doesn't say much for his trust in us that he won't sleep for fear we steal it."

"Have you seen how it moves sometimes?" said his comrade. "I reckon it's alive."

"Nah, it's treasure from that floating treasure house, Aeolia. That place is crammed from sea to sky with jewels off the seabed. Why else does it have that great wall round it and no way in for the likes of us? That bag's full of treasure, and he thinks that since we didn't see it given, we don't have a share in it. Well, let's see just what our noble captain's keeping to himself, shall we?"

Eurylochus crawled forward and twitched at the end of the silver cord. One man pulled on one end, one on another, a third man on the third loose end. Though the knot had seemed intricate and difficult to untie, it unraveled in a moment, and the neck of the bag fell open like a gaping mouth.

"What are you doing, you fools?" Odysseus sprang to

his feet. But his mutinous men could not hear what he shouted. Their arms were over their faces, and their hair streamed backward as a blast of wind hurled them against the mast and wrapped them in the splitting sail.

First came a golden west wind—strong but milky soft and heavy with the smell of Ithacan oleander. Next came a ragged east wind, full of tattered sea birds that swooped and screamed in their terrified ears—a green and nauseous wind that pitched the boat from one beam end to the other, then rolled them in sidelong troughs. Caught in its claws was the searing, red south wind, full of desert grit that scratched their faces and loaded down the twelve wallowing boats. Next came the north wind, white and whining, gray and groaning. It clapped the boats in ice so that they hung lower and lower in the heaving water. In pulling down the rags of sail, their hands froze to hemp and canvas alike.

The cowhide bag was whipped up off the deck and flew on a funnel of wind toward the milk-white sun. It started an avalanche of cloud tumbling down the sky, while winds from every point of the compass whirled and cavorted as far as the far horizon, then swooped back to ransack the boats. One wind was full of rain, one of hail. One was full of flying fish, another of crabs off beaches. One was white with lotus blossoms, and one was noisy with the shouts of Polyphemus still calling on his father, Poseidon: "Help me! Avenge me!"

And one wind plunged and bubbled into the ocean

then spouted up into the sky, hissing, "Die, Odysseus! Down, down, and drowning deep! Poseidon has spoken!"

It seemed a single moment later that his ship's heaving career through the mountainous seas was halted by a clang. The thwarts buckled and splintered, and the bulwark cracked in a dozen places as they were driven against a shining cliff of bronze. Odysseus saw his own face reflected there, the black-ringed eyes and the terror written in them. And he saw his twelve brave ships hammer against the bronze wall of Aeolia like hammers against a bell. Their crews beat on the shining wall with their fists and called out for King Aeolus to save them.

But they were there still when the winds subsided and the waves dispersed to the fringes of the blue carpeting sea and there was dead calm.

One head, and then thirteen more, looked over the golden parapet. "So! It is you, Lord Odysseus of Ithaca," said the king's voice.

"King Aeolus! Kind and generous friend. You'll help us, won't you? Gather up the winds, or lower down to us one gentle south-easterly breeze to carry us home! My men are exhausted. How are we to row such a way as the winds have blown us?"

But in reply, the king and queen and all their twelve children only tipped down the water from their washing bowls. "Go away, you godless man. This would never have happened if the gods were with you, if they wanted you to reach home. You've angered one of the

Immortals on high Olympus, and I won't offend them by helping you."

"But, my lord Aeolus! I did just as you told me! It was only the foolishness of my ignorant men that brought this disaster . . . this accident!"

"Accident, my lord Odysseus? This was no accident. Some voice has spoken against you in the halls of the gods. Get away from the walls of my bronze realm. You dull the shine with your ungodly breath!" And the king's head disappeared, behind his golden parapet, though his children stayed to spit the stones of olives down on the unhappy Greeks below.

The silence was broken only as, in each boat, forty oars rattled out between their thole-pins, and their wooden blades sliced white slits in the creamy ocean. For many days there was no sound but the creaking of wood and the drawing of weary breath, as the men heaved on their heavy oars.

When all their strength had gone and only shame remained to make them row, they looked up and saw the Land of the Laestrygonians.

There! A pair of breakwaters reached out like a pair of loving arms, and between them, a limpid harbor. Odysseus had his own boat hang back until all the others were safely berthed. Then, seeing there was no room for his vessel, he moored it by a single rope, outside the harbor mouth.

The green water was so clear that they could see every pebble, every weed, every crab on the seabed.

A tall young woman carrying a water jar on her head watched them from under her hand. She beckoned and waved her hand—a friendly girl, and someone you could call beautiful if she were not so uncommonly tall. Odysseus felt sorry for her, thinking how the other girls must make fun of her, and how a boy will shun a maiden who stands head and shoulders taller than him. He walked along the breakwater and began to introduce himself and his men, looking up into her beaming smile. In such a hospitable anchorage, they could not have met a more hospitable native.

"You must all come up to my father's palace," she said. "You see it up on the hill? He does so love to have people to supper."

Her father, she said, was King Lamus, and his palace was finer than any building Odysseus had ever seen. Its marble pillars stood taller than trees, its roof of porphyry spread out at the height where sea eagles stretch their wings, and curtains larger than sails blew in the upper windows. As the princess climbed the spiraling stairs of rosy onyx ahead of Odysseus, he laughed with delight at the magnificence round him and said, "I thought all the gods on Olympus had forgotten me. Now I see that they were planning new delights for me and my men."

His feet stumbled against the top step as the girl's

mother came out onto the gallery. "Well, Midget, and who have you brought home today?"

"Five hundred Greeks, Mama," said the princess. "Won't father be pleased?"

Her mother made the doorway she stood in look low. She could have dandled her little daughter on her knee, and if she had sat down on the shore, only a lighthouse could have saved sailors from shipwreck on her shins. Behind her came the king himself—eighty times bigger than Odysseus: the linen round his waist would have made tents for an army.

"Ah, supper!" he cried. For his daughter had spoken the truth. The king and all his kin liked nothing better than to have men to supper. Roasted or raw, cooked or still kicking.

King Lamus reached over the balustrade and grabbed up two men in the palm of one hand. Like the Cyclops, he savored his food.

Back down the onyx stairs, out from under the porphyry roof ran the Greeks, scattering this way and that. But the Laestrygonians had heard how King Lamus had fresh Greeks for supper. They had seen the boats in the harbor and were there on the waterfront, waiting.

Most of the Greeks reached their ships, dodging between the huge, sandaled feet of the giants, leaping their bulwarks and posting their oars with furious speed and deftness between their thole-pins. But the Laestrygonians simply took hold of each ship with finger and thumb, at the prow or by the anchor chain, lifted it up, and tipped out its crew of shrieking men.

Each giant carried a fishing spear, and with these they killed and killed and killed the helpless swimmers in the limpid water. Though some dived deep and some hid among the weeds, the Laestrygonians could see them through the clear green water and speared them with their long spears and ate them off the prongs. The empty boats they thrust prow-down into the silt.

Not one-half, not one-third, not one-tenth of the men threaded their steps between the giant feet and ran the length of the high harbor wall. Scarcely fifty men slipped between the darting prongs and leaped off the seaward side of the breakwater. There lay Odysseus's boat, moored only by its cable. And there Odysseus—last to flee—slashed the cable with his king's sword and leaped the widening gap as his men hauled on their heavy oars. He clutched the high stern, he tumbled his legs over the bulwark, and he dropped down beside the tiller. As he did so, his cockerel pecked at him angrily and put its head under its wing.

Forty-four wooden blades slashed white slits in the red ocean, and Odysseus steered for the open sea. He did not look back, for he knew that the harbor, with its two reaching arms, was no longer limpid-clear. Its waters ran red with spilled Ciconian wine from the smashed amphoras. And blood.

The sun went down, and the light poured thick as

honey along the quiet sea lanes. Night fell, and a million stars cascaded. But only fifty-two men of the five hundred who had set sail from Troy looked up and saw them.

Chapter Four

And This Little Piggy . . .

THE DOG STAR hung in the sky by night, and by day the bright discus of the sun flew overhead. But there was no knowing what course they wished to lay by either sun or moon. For Odysseus did not know where disaster had brought him. He steered to the west, always to the west, and northward, hoping to see the friendly profile of some Ionian isle. His men wept over their oars until it seemed the bilges ran with tears. And sometimes rain, cold and slighting, fell in Odysseus's face as if the gods were spitting on him. He uneasily watched the horizon, half expecting Poseidon to shoulder aside the blue main and shake his hair in the sky.

There! No, it was only the welling shoulder of a green promontory, lying along the horizon. The rowers pulled toward it with half-unwilling oars, for fear that this new landfall harbored some monster as ravenous as King Lamus or the appalling Cyclops.

But the ridged sea delivered them on diagonal waves onto the dark sand of a beach overhung by Alleppo pines. The long, green bristles were so heavily laden with cones that they looked to be full of birds, but there was no birdsong.

Odysseus said to his friend Polites, "I am putting half the crew under your command. Let's draw lots to see which half goes reconnoitering." So they shook stones—one black, one white—in a bronze helmet, and Polites drew out the black. Odysseus threw the helmet aside and clutched his comrade in his arms. "Take care, old friend. The stones themselves would shed tears if any harm came to you."

He watched the party of twenty-six men climb through the steep, piny path, grunting with exertion, the green spines catching in their cloaks or woollen jerkins. Half of him felt torn away.

On the black sand, his half-crew sat beneath the slatted shade of their oars and slept. But Odysseus, to shorten the waiting, went hunting and killed a stag to roast over an open fire.

The sun went down, and the low light poured thick as honey through the sea lanes and dry-land pathways. Still Polites and his men did not return. At that very moment when the sun falls beneath the sea with a flash of green, Eurylochus stumbled out of the trees, his hair spiny with pine needles, and his face a picture of fear.

"Aboard! Aboard!" He tried to shout, but his breath was spent, and his tongue was rigid with terror. It clacked in his jaws. He fell headlong in the black sand

and clutched Odysseus's feet. "Aboard or we're all pork, bacon, and brawn!"

Not until the sky was black and a million stars cascaded did Eurylochus recover enough to say what he had seen.

"We came to a house, a magnificent villa, with animal houses and vines and great curved doors hammered out of copper. We thought we were done for when a whole pack of wild animals came tearing round the house toward us. Not just boars, I don't mean, nor wild cats, nor wolves, but lions and black-furred cats as big as lions, with yellow eyes, and great striped beasts and golden ones spotted with black. We thought they'd tear us limb from limb! One of them leaped right up at me! . . . But they just pawed at us and licked our faces and rubbed their heads against our knees. I tell you, they were like little lap dogs, the way they fawned on us! The relief! Imagine it! And then we heard singing inside the house, and Polites called out, and the big copper doors swung open. . . ." Eurylochus halted, his eyes empty, his thoughts lost inside the house with the shining doors.

"Go on, man! What opened the doors? A monster? A magician?" demanded Odysseus.

"Oh, she's beautiful. More beautiful than any mortal woman you've ever seen. Circe she calls herself. She wears her hair in plaits that swing down behind her knees, and she carries a silver rod in her hand, and she smiles and smiles. . . . I don't know why I didn't follow the others when she beckoned them in. My legs were trembling so at the sight of her—and something inside me felt like a big brass anchor holding me back. As soon as they'd gone in, I regretted it. I ran up to the window to see what I was missing.

"She had a table laid already and high-backed seats for every man—as if she was expecting us. She pulled out footstools for each one to rest his feet on. I saw her creaming feta cheese with oil and honey and oregano and wine in a beautiful transparent bowl. Something else she added, too. . . . Something . . . something dreadful!" Eurylochus tore at his hair wildly. "I don't know what it was. Some herb with little flowers. I saw Demos, my friend Demos, troweling up the food with his fingers. He's always a great one for his food, and it did look so delicious! Then I saw him flinch a bit when the woman passed behind him and tapped him with her rod. She tapped everyone. Suddenly I thought, What's the matter with Demos's nose? It was flat, like a boxer's nose—and then like a snout. His eyes sank into his head, and the clothes fell off his back. Ach! His back was covered in bristles, and his legs were too short to balance him in his chair. He fell off onto the floor and onto his hands and knees—I mean onto his trotters. He was a hog, sir! A swine! A great grunting pig, and all the rest were like him."

"Even Polites?"

"Even him, sir. She drove them out through the back

doors and into the sties. I'm telling you, we weren't the first sailors ever to come here. She has boars and pigs and hogs more than they had in all Troy! It's dreadful to hear them. You can tell from the way they squeal and the look in their eyes that they have minds still, but they're all wrapped up in pig. And who's to spare them living out their natural lives like that—eating swill? Eh? It's the most horrible way the gods ever thought to punish us! And it's all your fault!"

Odysseus had already looped his longbow across his shoulder and was strapping on his sword. He stopped short and put his hand on the sword hilt, half drawing the blade. "What did you say, Eurylochus? What did you say?"

"I said it's all your fault for angering the great Earth-Shaker and Sea-Shifter, Poseidon. Now take us away from here before we're all turned into sucking pigs!"

The blue veins stood out on Odysseus's temples, and his knuckles whitened on the sword. But he controlled his temper and, turning his fiery eyes on the rest, said, "As soon as the sun is up, I am going to Circe's zoo to rescue my comrades or to die in the attempt. Let follow who dares, and let all craven cowards stay behind!"

The sorry crew followed Odysseus up through the Alleppo pines. Even Eurylochus, afraid to be left alone, fell in behind.

The morning sun splashed against Circe's great curving copper doors and hurt their eyes with its brightness.

Wild animals rushed out to greet them: leopards nuzzled them, a wolf wagged its tail, a tiger rolled in the path for its stomach to be tickled. And the hogs in the sties pressed against the gates, with heart-rending squeals.

Odysseus's men crouched alongside their bristly comrades and tried to comfort them, though the smell of the swill alone was sickening.

Odysseus alone stood in plain view of the shining doors, thigh-deep in the fragrant herbs that grew in vast variety round the house. Thyme and oregano, basil and rosemary, garlic and bay flourished all round. And twining in among them, the lovely but deadly delphinium and nodding mandragora. Odysseus looked down, and, between his two sandals, a little white flower was peeping out. It was a moli flower. He bent down, picked it, and pouched it—petals, root, and all—in his cheek. Just then, the great curved doors opened, and the sorceress Circe smiled at him.

She was as beautiful as the blue-trumpeted convolvulus that twined on Ithacan walls. Her hair hung down like the first rays of dawn, and her eyes were as clear and as green as . . . the harbor of Laestrygonia.

"Come in! Come in! You look weary. Look where I've prepared a seat for you, and a meal."

Indoors, he let her lift his feet onto the footstool beneath his chair and bring him a bowl of cheese creamed with honey and oregano and oil, and a cup of purple wine.

And he ate and drank it all.

Whap! She tapped him lightly on the shoulder with her slender rod of silver and, turning away, Circe said, "Now get to the sty with your comrades."

Odysseus sat back in his chair, crossed his ankles on the footstool, and patted his stomach. "Ah, delicious!" Circe's footsteps faltered. She looked over her shoulder.

She just had time to fall on her knees before Odysseus leaped across the table, sword drawn, and raised it two-handed over her head. "No! Don't strike, my lord Odysseus! You cannot kill me; I'm immortal. And besides, my dear, dear lord, you have no reason to hate me. I know you are Odysseus of Ithaca, for it was written in my horoscope at the moment of my birth that I should be conquered in heart and body by Odysseus, the greatest of the heroes of Troy!"

Odysseus spat out the shreds of the little moli flower that had saved him from her magic potion. "You ogress! You swineherd! You unnatural woman! How can I believe the words of a creature who defied all the natural laws of hospitality and made hogs out of my men? . . . Unless you swear by all the gods on Olympus to empty your heart of mischief."

"I swear! I swear! By all the gods and goddesses who ever saw the face of mighty Zeus: my mouth is yours with all its kisses; my arms are yours with all their embraces and with all their strength to help you; and my love is yours, bottomless as the Lake of Avothres in your own realm. . . . "

So Odysseus knotted his hand in her braided hair, kissed her on the mouth, and sheathed his sword.

She summoned five handmaidens—each as lovely as the stars in a constellation. And they brought wrappers of linen, ewers of water, jugs of wine, bowls of food, and music. Odysseus would have none of it—nor would he lie down on the soft, white bed Circe offered him—until his men were released from their misery.

Circe went to the sties, from sty to sty, anointing each bristly back with oil. Gradually, snouts, tails, ears, and hog hair melted away, and the pitiful Greeks found themselves kneeling in the muddy squalor of the pig run. They burst into tears, wagged their heads and hands in gratitude toward the heavenly gods, then looked about for their captain so as to bless him for saving them. But he had already gone. He was already behind the locked doors of the white and fragrant room to which Circe had led him by the hand.

She laid him on pillows and lambskin and cradled him in immortal arms.

Dawn, its tresses tumbling onto the bed, woke Odysseus. He sat up and looked out at the view. Beyond the herb garden were olive groves and orchards of lemons, apples, and limes. Vines entwined the marble colonnades, and hives shimmered with the early morning movement of bees. Tall, dark cypresses swayed like dancers, and the soft green of the pine forests was sprinkled with asphodels and orchids.

All he could see of the steely sea was a strip as long and narrow as a sword. Out there, the great Poseidon, Earth-Shaker and Sea-Breaker, who stood in the ocean trench and chewed the clouds with rage—out there he was waiting to cut off Odysseus.

I'll wait, thought Odysseus. Perhaps, in time, his anger will cool. And besides . . . this is a good place. It isn't Ithaca, but it is a good place. My men are tired, and I am tired. We need to rest.

And though men said of him that his body was a strung longbow and his wit the flying arrows, he unflexed the bow, and hung up the quiver of his cunning, and lay down again beside the sorceress Circe.

The Realm of Shadows

THE GRAPE HARVEST came, and the olive harvest, too. The season of winds passed by in the sky overhead, but on Circe's island there was never more than a breeze and a sprinkling of rain to make the greenery tremble. Circe's garden flourished by magic, by the watering of bright springs that she conjured from the ground—one day here, the next day there.

"There are springs and rivers on Ithaca, too," said Odysseus, "but without winter rains, it would be a brown, dry, dead place."

At the mention of his little, rugged island, a door banged somewhere in Odysseus's heart. The pages of his mind leafed over, and he glimpsed the face of his queen Penelope looking out to sea. But at the very first shadow of sadness, Circe kissed him with magic kisses, and his thoughts sank back into the soft pillows of her white and silver bed.

But when the thoughts of his men turned toward Ithaca, their wives, and their children, they had only the delights of the island to distract them. After a year, the sweetness of the melons no longer amazed them; the tenderness of the meat no longer satisfied the hunger within them. One morning, when Odysseus came out to breathe the morning air, Polites was standing by the door. He said, "Have you seen your men lately, my friend?"

"They always seem happy when I catch sight of them," replied Odysseus.

"They have eaten so well that their armor will not fasten. Their muscles are flabby for lack of use. What exercise do they get but to play with the leopards and walk the wolves? Every night they drink more than is good for them and get mawkish, and sing the old songs, and start talking about their dogs and farms and children. . . . They say you've forgotten Ithaca altogether—and Queen Penelope and your only son. They say you're happy to stay here in Circe's house till you die. I know that's not true. But how can I convince them? It's time to go, Lord Odysseus. It's time to go."

Odysseus looked over his shoulder at the trestle where his king's sword lay tarnishing and his bronze helmet served for a bowl to keep figs in. "You're right, Polites. I know it in my heart. Tell the men to make ready the boat: mend the sail, retouch the paint, rub the oars with linseed oil. Tomorrow morning we shall set sail for Ithaca. I'll go now and ask Circe to direct us on our way. With her magic arts and the knowledge of a goddess, she must know where Ithaca lies."

"Be careful, my lord. Don't let her tempt you into changing your mind."

"Polites, have a care. I am Odysseus of Ithaca, hero of Troy! If I decide to go, no woman is going to prevent me."

And when Circe saw the look on Odysseus's face, she knew at once that his heart was set on going. "With my magic arts and the knowledge entrusted to me as a goddess, I could tell you where Ithaca lies. I could teach you what stars to follow and where to keep the noonday sun as you steer. But I am forbidden. My heart forbids me, but more than that, the gods on Mount Olympus forbid it. And I cannot tell you what winds will blow. I cannot know what miseries Poseidon has in store for you. And I am forbidden to know whether all or any of you will ever reach home alive. Oh, Odysseus! Think again! Stay in the safe harbor of my two arms. . . . No, I can see it's useless to speak of safety to a hero. Well, and are you hero enough to go where you must, for the directions you need? Are you? Because the man I'll send you to can tell you about more than your journey across the sea. He can tell you about your journey from birth to death: every second and syllable of your life."

Then Odysseus trembled from head to foot, as he had trembled when he saw the great Achilles carried off the battlefield at Troy with an arrow in his heel and the astonishment of death in his eyes. "There was a man—a soothsayer—everyone has heard of: Tiresias of Thebes. If he were alive, you would have sent me to him. But he's dead long since. Who else?"

"No one else," said Circe. "Tiresias is the man I mean. You must look for him in Hades."

His knees buckled under him, and Odysseus felt his heart clamor against his ribs. His vital organs melted in the sweat of terror. "No living man in the history of the world has been down to the Realm of Shadows!"

"You have forgotten Hercules, my friend, who borrowed the great dog Cerberus as one of his Labors. And Orpheus who went there to fetch back his beloved Eurydice when the god of the Underworld stole her away."

"But Orpheus failed!"

"Then you must not fail. Oh, Odysseus, Odysseus, my love! You need not fetch anything or anyone out of the Realm of Shadows. You need only the advice of old Tiresias. Do you have the courage for such a journey?"

Odysseus's men had prepared the boat to set sail, but then lain down for their afternoon rest, when their captain came leaping down the beach calling to them. "To your oars, men! And bring aboard only one perfect ram, a black sheep, and food enough for three nights at sea!"

Bleary eyed, the men jostled on the beach. "Where are we going, then?"

"Not to Ithaca?"

"A trial voyage for the boat, my lord?"

49

"They're sacrifices. Why are we loading sacrifices?"

"Where's Elpenor?" demanded Odysseus. "Is he drunk again? Good-for-nothing waster. He moves as fast as a tortoise, and that's too fast for his brain to keep up. They say he was so stupid in battle that the Trojans didn't know whether to shoot him or make oars out of him. We used to call him "'Elpless Elpenor. Where is he? Well, we'll sail without him. . . ." And by complaining ceaselessly, incessantly about the missing Elpenor, Odysseus managed to put to sea without answering their questions. Wooden blades sliced white slits in the creamy ocean. The boat leaped forward. But on the stern rail, the captain's old cockerel sat huddled in its cloak of wings and made not a sound.

They followed Circe's directions to the last syllable, taking for their pointer the sword that hung in the sky from the belt of starry Orion. Through the smooth and colorful sea ran a trough of gray, turbulent water: the current called River Ocean. Into and along this, the boat was drawn irresistibly. Their oars speeded them, but the River Ocean guided them, until mist from the cauldron sea curled over their heads and nothing was visible of the sky. There was a smell in the fog—half sea, half land—and a noise of waves breaking. The rowers snatched in their oars as the boat slid under a narrow arch of rock. They snatched in their fingers as the boat squeezed, with not a hand's breadth to spare, into a tunnel of clammy granite.

"What place is this you've brought us to?" demanded Eurylochus, and his voice boomed and re-echoed up and down the passageway.

"It's the sea lane to the Underworld," said Odysseus. "Our solitary hope of finding our way home. If it had not been necessary, I would not have brought you here."

Then Eurylochus fell on his knees in the bottom of the boat, and the rest of the men let out such a wail of despair that its echoes hammered in their heads for an hour after.

There was no need of oars: the flow of River Ocean carried them on. When they reached out their fingers in the darkness, they felt the slime on the walls, and sometimes a smoothness like hair or the flinching softness of a face. Night was absolute, but no stars cascaded. Then the walls widened, and the echoes of their crying soared into the vault of an over-arching cavern as high as the dome of King Lamus's palace.

In impenetrable darkness, the boat beached on drifts of decaying seaweed, whose invisible ooze closed over the men's feet and ankles as they stepped out. A phosphorescent glow drew them to the mouth of a second sloping tunnel. It sloped so steeply that their leather sandals slipped; the surefooted ram and sheep almost escaped them. At the foot of the slope, one man cannoned into another. Punches were exchanged. Then the sailors looked round them . . . and saw the faces of the dead, watching.

They were in a vast cavern as high almost as the

dome of the sky itself. Night was absolute. But a million white faces teemed through the gloom, trooping toward Odysseus and his men with outstretched arms and reaching fingers; their lips shaped words they had no breath to speak. They filled the cavern; they climbed down the uneven blackness of the walls; they hung like bats from the over-arching roof.

Snatching his king's sword from his thigh, Odysseus killed the black ram and the sheep with one stroke, and their blood made a phosphorescent pool on the cavern floor. Like jewels set in the solid darkness, a million eyes gleamed with delight. Far from falling back, the ghosts rushed forward with a noise like the sails flapping on a sunken ship.

"Stop! These beasts are sacrifices to the god Pluto!" yelled Odysseus. "None may drink the blood who has not been invited to feast with me, the servant of Pluto and of mighty Zeus!"

The eyes of the dead remained on the blood—wistful and longing—and their sighs lifted Odysseus's hair.

That was when he saw Elpenor—not fat and grinning, as he usually was, but pasty-faced and solemn, standing apart from the rest. His limbs and armor and hair were frayed out to merest shreds: the suggestion of a body. And his head was twisted awkwardly on his shoulders.

"You're here ahead of us. How, Elpenor? You weren't in the boat. I know you weren't at your oar!"

"No, master. I was here already, sir. You see I was

sleeping on the roof when you called us. I jumped up and went to climb down the ladder. But I forgot, you see. I forgot where I'd put the ladder on the way up. Yes, comical, wasn't it? Over I went and landed on my head. And my neck was broken. But nobody noticed. Nobody missed me. No one came looking for me. "'Elpless Elpenor, you all said, I suppose. And I'm there now. At least my name is—wedged inside my body. Nobody buried me, you see. Nobody called my name across the water. So I don't have one here."

"You don't have a name?" said Odysseus. He wanted to reach out and comfort Elpenor, but there was nothing to take hold of.

"The spirits don't know my name, so they can't speak to me. And I can't tell them my name, because they can't hear me. Ha-ha! I'm No Wun, you see, Lord Odysseus. Just like you were, in the cave of the Cyclops." It was horrible to see a ghost laugh so joylessly.

"We shall bury your body, Elpenor. If we live to see daylight again, we shall go back and give you all the honors of a soldier and a sailor. I swear it, by the all-powerful Zeus, master of the gods."

"If you would . . . if you would . . ." The boy's voice seemed to come from the bottom of a deep well, and his face diminished as he backed away to the size of a pinhead. But in going, he led Odysseus's eye toward a woman. Hard to recognize a woman after thirteen years. Even your own mother.

"Is it? Can it be you?" But the ghost's eyes rested not on Odysseus, but longingly on the pool of sacrificial blood. "Come forward, Anticleia, daughter of Autolycus, wife of Laertes, and feast with your son!" called Odysseus, though his voice broke with emotion. The female ghost fluttered to the pool of blood and drank from it. "Mother! Mother! Are you dead, then? Can it be true that you're not tending your lambs and sewing covers for the beds of Pelicata Palace?"

The ghost stared into Odysseus's eyes and lifted her hands toward his face, but without touching him. "How long can an old woman live on hopes and wishes, Son? You did not come and you did not come and you did not ever come home. I didn't have the patience of your dear wife, Penelope. And I hadn't the courage of your dear son, Telemachus. My old heart broke with grief: I was so sure that you were dead. . . . And I was right, too, surely—because here you are, in the Realm of Shadows."

"But I'm alive, Mother! I'm alive! I strayed into strange waters, and I'm here to ask directions from old Tiresias of Thebes. Oh, Mother, couldn't you have waited for me just one more year, just a few more . . . ?"

"Who spoke my name?" A tall spirit—taller by a hand's span than any of the rest—parted the hosts of the dead as he bore down on Odysseus.

The other Greeks fell on their hands and knees and sobbed hysterically, saying, "We'll never leave here!"

"Pluto will hull our souls like peas!"

"Who will call our names over the ocean? We'll be nameless forever!"

"I, Odysseus of Ithaca, spoke your name, Tiresias—I, who have braved the belly of Hell to ask your advice—I, who was directed here by Circe the goddess, whose hair is like the first rays of dawn and whose fate it was to help me! Come forward and feast with me!"

"Hmm. Achilles was right. He told me when he came here, white with the astonishment of death, that you were a . . . remarkable man, Odysseus." When Tiresias spoke, his puckered, drawstring lips did not move. His voice seemed to come from the center of his breastbone. "You are heartless, too, to disturb the immortal drifting of my spirit. Not since my days of flesh have I vexed myself with other people's lives, other people's futures. Well, well, what is it you want to know?"

"From Circe's magical isle, how must I steer to reach Ithaca?"

When Tiresias spoke at last, he spoke of stars and tides, of islands and shoals, of the singing Sirens and the Wandering Rocks, of Scylla Six-Headed and Charybdis the Hole. And last of all he spoke of the Island of Helios. He spoke so softly that only Odysseus could hear. And he spoke secrets that might have been sold for diamonds to the sea captains of the world. The hero's hair stirred in the nape of his neck when he heard of the dangers ahead, but he did not allow his voice to tremble when he said, "Circe, maiden of the plaited hair, said that you could tell me more—more than the course of my voyage home over the world-encircled sea."

"Did she? Did she?"

"She said you could tell me the voyage of my life, from birth to death: not just what's gone before, but things to come as well. Shall we reach home alive?"

The seer turned his face away. Still, his voice emerged from the fumy regions of his ghostly back, but Odysseus could not see the look on his face. "If you steer the course I have told you, if you take the precautions I have told you, above all if . . . "

"If! If! Shall I reach home or not?"

"There are choices to be made, young man. How can I know what you will choose in your foolishness, or what fate your foolish men will choose for you? If you do not let them slaughter the Cattle of the Sun, you will reach Ithaca again. Your wife will welcome you, your son will listen to your stories, and the suitors will be driven out of Pelicata Palace."

"Who? What suitors? What are you talking about, old man?"

The ghost turned back toward Odysseus wearily. "Even now, young men are beaching their boats in the three bays of Ithaca. 'Odysseus is dead,' they tell your queen. 'Admit it and do not waste your beauty in waiting for a dead man. Marry one of us. Marry and make a king for Ithaca. For what good is a dead king to his kingdom, and what good is a kingdom without a king?' So say the suitors."

Odysseus let fly such a roar of disgust that the spirits' diaphanous bodies fluttered in the draft. He drew his king's sword and wielded it round his head. "I'll cut their blood from their flesh and their flesh from their bones!" he raged.

But dead men don't flinch at the sight of a sword's blade or the fury of a living man. The host of ghosts began to drift away.

"Come, men! There's no time to waste. I must be in Ithaca before the next moon wanes! There are rats in my granary and maggots in my vines! What? Haven't you seen enough of the Underworld? There'll be time enough to see every room of it when you're dead!"

His men needed no second telling. They fled on skidding sandals up the sloping passageway to the impenetrable dark, the water, and the smell of seaweed. They could not drift back the way they had come, because the flow of River Ocean was against them— down, always down—so they felt and pulled their way, sliding their hands over the slimy softness of the walls.

Against the flow of River Ocean they pulled their boat through, until it nosed out into the brightness of morning. Dawn was dancing in flowery cloth-of-gold against the eastern sky, and her unbraided tresses curled across the water. It was the most beautiful sight the men of Ithaca had ever seen. And if the rugged green of their little island home had rested then on the horizon, each and every man would have lived forever.

Chapter Six

Sorrow and Singing

"OH, TELEMACHUS!" CRIED Queen Penelope to her handsome son. "Is he really dead and under the sea? Or in some distant land? Am I a widow, and are you left fatherless? If I knew! If only I knew!"

"I'm sure he's alive, Mother. I'm sure the gods will bring him safely home to us. Do please be patient for just a little while longer."

"Oh, I have patience, Telemachus. More than the sea has that pounds on a rock to make sand. But how am I to drive off these suitors? They eat our food and drink our wine and they tell me, 'Odysseus is dead! Ithaca has no king. Marry me! Marry me! Marry one of us!'"

"I'll fight them, then, and drive them away—every last one of them! They only want father's crown and gold and palace and flocks and to be king of Ithaca."

Penelope stroked her son's hair (it reminded her so much of Odysseus's own brazen curls) and said soothingly, "You're still only a boy, Telemachus, and they are looking for an excuse to kill you. You can't fight them all:

there are thirty or more of them with their feet on the tables and their noses in the vats! If I must be patient, so must you."

But Telemachus leaped up and seized his father's spear, which stood against the wall. "At least I can go and look for my father. Zeus knows, I was too young when he left to remember his face, but someone somewhere must know what has become of him. I'll travel to the mainland and seek out the men who fought with him at Troy. If I have to, I'll climb Olympus itself and ask the gods what has become of him! Perhaps I'll come home with good news. Perhaps I'll even come home with Odysseus himself to save you from these sandflies!" And he was gone, all at once, to muster a crew of the few good men he could trust, who tended their sheep in Ithaca's wild places.

"The goddess Athene go with you!" called his mother after him. "And may she guide you to my dear Odysseus!"

The hero's name echoed down the empty corridors of the palace, hollow and lonely and sad. And Penelope turned back to the window. The little harbor below was full now of brightly painted boats. With every tide another arrived . . . but never the king's ship. Only more suitors to harry her with threats and wheedling. Perhaps it was true what they told her: that Odysseus would not come and would not come and would not ever come, that his soul was already pining in the Realm of Shadows. And now her only son was setting off across the heartless sea, whose waves were always arriving, always coming home to the shores of Ithaca, but always with empty arms.

From the mouth of Hell, Odysseus returned to moor his brightly painted boat in the harbor of Circe's magic island, while the pine-scented air was thick as honey with the low light of evening. They found the body of Elpenor, sprawled in the shadow of the house, with a gentle panther keeping watch beside him and brushing off the flies with his long, black tail.

His comrades buried him in his armor beneath a mound of earth and honored him with all the rites of death. Odysseus himself dragged the heavy oar that was Elpenor's from the ship to the top of the mound and drove it into the soft earth. And Odysseus himself called the man's name three times over the striped and brimming ocean: "Elpenor! Elpenor! Elpenor!"

When he climbed down, Circe stood waiting with a cup of wine and meat. "Well? And did Tiresias answer all your questions?"

"He told me the terrors that lie ahead. But nothing can equal the sights of the Underworld itself. Whether I stand or lie down, whether I fight or run, whether I stay here or try to reach Ithaca—one day I must dwindle down into a flag of mist and live in the dark forever, and my name will be forgotten on the Earth. What terror can compare with what I've seen?"

"Then stay here with me, Odysseus, and I shall keep you from death for a hundred years."

For a moment Odysseus hesitated. Then he shook himself, and the fear flew off him as the water flies off an otter's fur. "I must set sail. I've a mind to hear the Sirens' song in the morning."

"You reckless man, Odysseus," said the goddess bitterly. "Do you think, because Athene gave you a body taut like a bow and a mind as quick as arrows, that you can listen to the Sirens and live? For as long as ships have sailed, the Sirens have sat on their rock and sung. A bare, bald rock it is, heaped up with the bones of sailors. Each one of those sailors has heard the singing of the Sirens and leaned on the rails to listen. First he has thought, 'What a sweet sound.' And then he has thought, 'I must hear more.' And then he has thought, 'What a waste of my life not to have spent it here, listening!' And then he has thought, 'I'll die if I leave this singing!' And then he has died—long and lingering—his ship foundering on the barren rock and his body sprawled at the feet of the Sirens, starving in his ecstasy and parching in his rapture and loathing himself for his foolishness. You think you and your Greeks are different, but mortal men are all the same when it comes to the Sirens' singing."

Odysseus held up his hands as if he surrendered to her greater wisdom. But in his eyes she saw the gleam of mischief.

"Oh, you self-willed, headstrong man, Odysseus! Go to my beehives and take the wax from the combs. Knead it and slice it and seal the ears of all your men. Then have them tie you to the mast with rope. And tell them when you beg to be released, to tie you tighter still, and with more rope. Now, say good-bye, and let it never be said by gods or mortal men that I did not help you all I could!"

Then Odysseus kissed her and laughed out loud and said, "When they sing my story on Ithaca, I'll have them call you the goddess of magic powers, whose hair hangs down in golden braids like the first rays of dawn, wise as the bees and as sweet as honey. I shall remember you, Circe, whenever my hives are overflowing!"

He boarded his brightly painted ship and stood at the prow, his cockerel on his arm, and four dozen wooden oars sliced white slits in the creamy sea. The sail hung down, hungry for wind.

Warily he kept watch for the Island of the Sirens. There! Was that birdsong or human voices drifting toward him? Either way, a sweet sound to hear at sea. He kneaded the wax; the heat of the morning sun had made it soft. He stopped up the ears of his men, one by one, and all the while the music grew louder.

Too quiet, too low. I must get closer, he thought, and stood with his hand to his ear on the dipping prow. It was Polites who roped him round and round and tied the rope ends to the mast.

63

"What are you doing?" said Odysseus irritably, mouthing the words at deaf Polites.

"Only what you would have commanded me if it had not slipped your mind, my lord. I heard Circe's advice."

Come, my sisters, come and see
How the world-encircled sea
And slow tide of purple time
Have brought, at last, the one sublime
Fast vessel we
Have longed to see—
The Odyssey. . . .

"Circe lied. She said the island was bare and barren. But it's covered over in flowers—orchids and lilies and bougainvilleas. . . . "

See how his head is crowned with curls;
See how his sail, all unfurled
Hangs empty out of pity—
For though some call us pretty,
Loneliness
Tortures us,
Odysseus. . . .

"Everyone lied! They said the Sirens were harpies, with the bodies of vultures and the heads of women. But they're lovely! Lovelier than the orchids or the lilies or the bougainvilleas . . . lovelier than Ithaca. How would my crabbed, aging wife look alongside them—their shoulders so white, their eyes so imploring. Poor ladies! What manner of man would I be to spurn them? Polites, untie me!"

Ah! When the world pronounced your name,
Why did they not speak of the flames
Of glory that round you wreath?
The gods forbid that you should leave.
What happiness
Remains unless
You swim to us,
Odysseus?

"Polites! Can't you see? Circe lied to us. Let me go this instant! I command you!"

But Polites's shoulders were hunched over his oar: he could not hear, and if he looked up, his eyes did not linger on Odysseus's twisted mouth. "Polites! You'd better do as I say or I'll kill you afterward for defying me! Untie me!"

But Polites turned his head away so as not to look into Odysseus's face on every backward pull of the oar.

"You other men! Listen! The man who frees me can have Polites's rank! Any of you—look at me! Whoever frees me can have Ithaca. Take it. How can I rule Ithaca when I'm needed here? Don't you hear what they're saying? They've waited centuries just for me! Men! Look up! TAKE THE WAX OUT OF YOUR EARS! Cut me free, I beg you. Look! The distance isn't so far. I could swim across! You go on if you must: take the boat; I shan't need it. But cut me free and let me swim. Look, the distance is getting wider. For the love of all the gods—have pity on me! Someone! What are you? Pieces of rock? Does it please you to see the hero of Troy reduced to tears? Don't you know what pity is?"

Then Polites leaped up from his thwart and, with his eyes turned away from Odysseus's face, he fetched another coil of rope and wound it round and round and round both man and mast, from ankle to throat, from throat to ankle. All the while, Odysseus begged, pleaded, and sobbed, pulled grotesque, piteous faces, plunging from rage to craven tears as the weather alternated between lightning and drizzling rain.

When he had done, Polites sat down on the heaving deck. Only one gap in the coils of rope allowed the king's right hand to reach and claw at him. Polites took the hand in his and held it, though Odysseus's furious grip squeezed like a wine press. Deafly he watched the silent mouth contort, and he watched the veins beat in his captain's temples in time with the strokes of the plunging oars.

At last the grip relaxed. Odysseus's head fell forward on his chest, and large tears splashed down onto Polites's hair. Over the starboard quarter, the Island of the Sirens dipped out of sight below the brimming horizon. Polites took the wax out of his ears, fetched a knife, and cut free Odysseus, whose body was ringed round with the marks of the hempen rope. In a small and faltering voice he asked, "What did you see, Polites?"

"Three hideous vultures with horny talons and the heads of women. An acre of jagged rocks where nothing grew except white trees of bone that used to be good men. What did you see, my lord?"

But the question was never answered, for a headwind brought a fine gray spume and the sound of distant roaring.

"Unstop the men's ears, Polites, and let the tillerman take an oar. I'll steer, myself."

"Why? What is it, my lord?"

"If Circe and Tiresias spoke the truth, we are about to see the greatest terrors of the undiscovered world."

67

Chapter Seven

Snake-Headed Scylla and Charybdis the Hole

FOUR DOZEN TAPERED and polished blades splashed into the troughing sea as the men dropped their oars. The sea was a dark, slate gray, like the tiled roof of some endless ocean palace. Somewhere beneath that roof, Poseidon sat.

"Don't give up, men!" cried Odysseus, cheerfully striding the length of the boat, up and down between their slumping shoulders. "This is not like Laestrygonia or the Land of the Cyclops! We aren't flying like sparrows into traps! I know what lies ahead. Didn't we travel to Hades for the knowledge? Tiresias told me! Ahead of us on the port side are the Wandering Rocks. No ship has ever passed under their shadow and sailed out again. No speed of rowing, no following wind could drive us through with speed enough to escape destruction. So? A simple choice, then! We must keep to the starboard side of the channel, hard by the smooth-faced cliff. . . . "

"We're sailing toward Charybdis—Charybdis the Hole!" cried Eurylochus, his jaws clattering with fright.

"Yes, and if we time our passage carefully, we shall pass Charybdis when it's full of sea. Courage, men! Aren't we loved by the goddess Athene herself? And didn't we row down to the Underworld to prepare us for this trip? What must I do to put the fire back into your hearts? Must I put on the armor I wore at Troy? All right. Here! The golden breastplate and the brace of bronze. And here! The bronze helmet on my head, so that the gods will see the sun dazzle on it and know where we are! Now split the ocean with your polished oars so that the gods may stand in admiration of your speed!"

Between every thole-pin the oars rattled, and four dozen wooden blades sliced white slits—white trenches—in the creamy ocean. But Polites said under his breath, "My lord, Tiresias warned you that no armor and no sword would stave off Scylla."

"Did you hear the words he spoke, then, Polites? Did the others hear them?"

"Only you and I, my lord. And you are right to leave the men in ignorance. If they knew that Scylla was waiting, no words or whips would drive them through this channel."

The words between them were washed away by salt spray, and wisps of smoke smudged the sparkling air. A noise of avalanches reached them through a screen of smoke, and, little by little, they could make out a movement.

For a moment it seemed that the sea was solid and

only the land was moving. Travelers speak of reaches in the sea where ice floats mountain-high, always cracking and rending itself, while palaces of snow slide into the water down rivers of frozen sea. History speaks of the Earth splitting open and bleeding molten fire through its wounds, blacking out the sun with ash and drowning whole kingdoms in fire. But no one could have put words to the sight that greeted Odysseus and his men.

Towers of rock, sky-high, writhed shoulder to shoulder for as far as the eye could see, grinding together their crags and precipices, striking sparks from the flint. Boulders big as bullocks stirred and rocked—as loose as an old man's teeth—then toppled and bowled down the cliff face to shatter the sea. Gouts of lava spouted from every crevice, snatching sea birds off the wing and dissolving all trace of them. Along the cliff's stony roots, the sea boiled blood-red. The channel was peppered with dead and dying fish. The hull's timbers began to bow as it furrowed through the boiling water. Steam condensed on scalded faces and ran down like sweat or tears.

Hard over to starboard they rowed, hard over as far from the Wandering Rocks as they could go . . . so hard over that their starboard oars clattered against the base of the opposite cliff. A sheer, smooth cliff it was, as smooth as the walls of Aeolia, as smooth as the forehead of Athene herself. Not a ledge, not a crevice, not even a tuft of grass to give a man footholds to climb up. The top was out of sight. But higher than an archer could shoot an arrow, they could glimpse the dark mouth of a cave. . . .

"Are we close to Charybdis yet, Captain?" asked one of the men. They dared not look over their shoulders to see the way they were going. They could already hear the crashing of water.

"Not yet, not yet. Not till this smooth cliff drops down lower and a fig tree juts out—that marks where Charybdis opens its mouth. Courage, men! Sound carries. We're not close to Charybdis yet."

His men's eyes were on him. They saw Scylla first, reflected in the bronze of his helmet. He saw that they had seen her and said, "Bend your heads to your chests and row! Whatever you see, whatever you hear, just look to your oars and row!"

Odysseus drew his king's sword, thinking to defend his men or die in the attempt. But when she came, there was no defense against Scylla.

Liars tell of monstrous squid that rise from the ocean trench to wrap great ships in their embrace and drag them down to devour them in lairs of water and bone. But no liar could have invented the beast that came out of that cave.

Above their heads, she snaked her six necks. She cast a shadow like a many-stranded whip, each knotted end the size of a fist. But the shadow grew—larger and larger— on the boat's deck. The Scylla's heads were not the size of fists. They were not the size of melons. They were not

71

the size of drums. The Scylla's heads were larger even than the fist of King Lamus, who ate men out of his palm. Each mouth was the size of a slimy cave. And set in her jaws, like stalactites and stalagmites, were six rows of rending teeth. Her teeth were as many as the blood vessels in a man's body: vessels she loved to break, along with bone and muscle and heart.

With each head she lifted a man, pulling him from under his oar. Six heads, six mouths, six men calling on the gods for deliverance. Six heads, six mouths, and six sons of Ithaca weeping their last for their wives and children. Six heads, six mouths, and six dead men, each with Odysseus's name on his lips, begging to be spared. Six heads, six mouths, but not a limb or head or reaching hand or shrieking left, for the Scylla had devoured her catch and was coiling herself back into the bloody recesses of her cave to digest her meat. Though she had lived for centuries, her only purpose on the surface of the Earth was to ambush and to eat and to sleep.

"Row, men, row! Shut your ears and your eyes and row till we are out of reach of the Scylla, or she may strike again!"

Then Odysseus was glad of his king's helmet with its long nosepiece and cheeks of bronze. For it hid the pallor of his face and the terror, and it hid his tears, too, which flowed like blood. He looked at his king's sword and the six blunted crescents in its shining blade where he had hacked at the scaly neck of the writhing Scylla.

He shook his head and plugged up his ears, but the voices went on ringing inside his head, even though they had been long since silenced: "Save us, Odysseus! Save us!"

Only the sound of Charybdis could drown out those voices.

Charybdis was a Hole. Charybdis was a mouth. Charybdis was a gill in the throat of the fishy ocean. When the ocean breathed in, water and air, flotsam and jetsam, weeds and waves, fish and birds were sucked into its gaping pit and spun deeper and deeper than the deepest well in the world, whirled round in a spiral of sea. And when the ocean breathed out, water and air, flotsam and jetsam, scale and feather were belched out again in gouts of sea like the foam from a mad dog's mouth.

Twice in every tide, the whirlpool sucked down every atom of water and floating morsel—as deep as the seabed itself. Twice in every tide, it expelled all that it had sucked in, but for a perpetual litter which circled forever in its vortex.

The first sight they had of Charybdis was the tall mast of a ship, circling, circling, circling—as though an invisible god was stirring the water with it. The noise was of ripping canvas and cataracts of sea, of the cowhide bag of Aeolus unfastened beneath the surface. They could not make themselves heard above it; they could not hear their own thoughts; and when they breathed, they breathed in flying spray.

"Is the tide right?" they mouthed at Odysseus through the smoke of spume. "Shall we be sucked down?"

"Row!" cried Odysseus. "If the gods wish it, Charybdis will breath out and let us pass. If the gods don't . . . " They could not hear him above the racketing of Charybdis. All they could see was the brightness of his eyes in the arches of the king's helmet and the twisting of his mouth beneath the nosepiece. And they could feel the boat slip sideways beneath them, dragged toward the spiral trough of Charybdis. The six oars of the six dead men were sucked through their pins and bounded toward the whirling pit.

Then—as it seemed they must surely glide sideways over the glassy rim—there was a sudden silence, a moment's silence, as in the mind of a dying man. The solid, glassy rim of Charybdis shattered and, with a gurgling confusion, the waters leveled. The broken shipwreck floating at its center paused for a moment. They could see every open slat. They could see every gap in the ribs of the skeleton crew who sat at its oars.

The next moment the shipwreck began to swing the other way. The coil of Charybdis was rewinding . . . the other way. The waves spun, and, at the center of the coil, the water dipped like a saucer, dipped like a dish, dipped like a bowl, dipped like a trough.

"Row!" cried Odysseus, and they sped onward with their polished oars flashing like beams of sun. "Row!"

Charybdis, breathing in, grew as deep as a cave, as

74

deep as a well, but the boat of the Greeks was skimming beyond the reach of its centripetal pull. They were past. They were unwrecked. They were alive!

Beneath the bronze nosepiece of the king's helmet, they could see Odysseus's teeth flash white as he grinned. And when the noise of Charybdis died away, he was still repeating, "Well rowed! Rowed like true men of Ithaca!"

As they looked beyond him, they could still see the tip of the mast of the dead ship spinning.

The Most Important Promise of All

THE GOLDEN SEA was studded with jewels of sunlight too bright and too many to count.

Three times Odysseus called the name of each man eaten by Scylla. Three times he shouted their names over the sea. But there were no oars to plant on the shore in memory. There was no shore to plant them in, nor a place to sacrifice Circe's black sheep in gratitude to the gods.

There! Their dazzled eyes were able to make out the grassy slopes of an island from the circlet of clouds on the horizon. Odysseus screwed up his eyes against the brightness. "Tiresias of Thebes spoke the truth! We've reached the country of Helios!"

The men looked up and smiled ill-fitting smiles. Fright had changed the shape of their faces.

"I know what you're thinking," said Odysseus, "but put it out of your minds. You're thinking, here's a sheltered mooring for a night's sleep and a bite of food. But we won't set foot on Helios. I say lean on your oars, and let's put it far behind us before sunset."

A murmur of discontent ran along the boat. Reproachful eyes scowled at Odysseus. The rhythm of the oars faltered, and the blades halted in the air, like the feathers of a forlorn sea bird. Eurylochus got up, his feet splayed across the keel of the boat. "And I say we stop and rest. We're not all superhuman like you. We're not all heroes with leather for muscles and fire for blood. We're just poor mortals. We get tired. We get very, very tired and we need to sleep. We don't enjoy sleeping over our oars while you stretch out on the quarter-deck in half a mile of cloak. We don't relish waiting for a storm to come up out of the darkness like a fist and smash us to splinters or shovel water over our heads. We don't care much for a man who knew about Scylla and chose not to tell us. Six of us have died today cursing the name of Odysseus, who can't even spare the time to give them funeral rites. To put it briefly, Captain, we don't care to row on past Helios. It looks like an excellent place to spend the night."

Odysseus put his hand to the hilt of the king's sword, but the tiller swung and nudged him off balance as all the men stood up at their oars and began to stamp their feet. They were applauding Eurylochus.

"You foolish . . . What's it to me where we drop anchor? We can all walk home our separate ways to

Ithaca, if that's what pleases you. I was just concerned, in case Eurylochus here was too weak-willed to resist the temptation of roast beef. Because, as you know, if any one of you so much as lays a finger on the Cattle of the Sun, we can all look forward to death and destruction."

The purple veins throbbed in Odysseus's temples, but a hundred fingers were drumming on the oars of the ship. Insolent eyes glared at him. "Captain," said Polites softly, "we have enough grain aboard to keep us in bread for a week—a black sheep, too, and honey from Circe's hives. I think you'll find that the men can resist the temptation for just one night."

Odysseus did not answer, but threw the tiller over sharply, so that the boat veered toward the Island of Helios. The cockerel on the stern rail reeled and reached out a grasping claw to keep itself from falling.

The surf was heavy. It slammed them down on the pebbles of the beach and boiled round their chests as they pulled the boat up higher. The island had no lee shore, for it had no hill of any height, and the winds blew over it and set the grass tossing and rolling, shaking free seeds like the white spray from the crests of waves.

When the sun went down and light poured thick as honey along the sea lanes, it found no dry-land pathways to wander in. The only branches were the branching horns of the sun god's beautiful cattle.

Their silken hides gleamed russet red in the sunset,

and their great brown eyes blinked at its brightness. When the sunbeams stroked their backs, their withers twitched and their stocky legs stamped and their long tails swished seed-heads out of the white, autumnal dandelions. Their curving horns were as long as the king's bow.

Odysseus's men fetched the black sheep Circe had given them and the sack of ground grain, and they ate roast lamb and doughy bread. Night fell, but instead of a million stars, rain cascaded out of the sky, and behind it came the wind.

"Where would we be now if we'd stayed at sea?" said Eurylochus smugly, and the rest agreed with him.

They overturned the boat on the beach and sat beneath it, chewing on their bread. Then they wrapped themselves in their cloaks and went to sleep or lay awake and listened to the drumming of the rain and the lowing of the cattle trampling the wet grass into the mud.

Next morning it was still raining, and the sea hurled itself up the beach like a chained dog lunging with white teeth at an unwelcome visitor. The Greeks did not so much as put out their heads from under the upturned boat, though it was dark underneath it, and the sun's cattle chewed on the ropes.

Next morning it was still raining, and the lightning, like barbed Trojan arrows, wounded the sky and set it growling. The Greeks lay on their stomachs, chewing on their bread, and watched the raindrops quarry holes in the beach.

After a week, all the grain that Circe had given them was gone. They did not want for water. It trickled out of the bilges, it leaked between the boards, it condensed out of their steamy breath against their chilly skin. But all their food was gone.

Odysseus wandered the island from north to south, west to east, and returned with the leather of his skirt double its weight with water, his hair plastered to his neck with rain, the hairs of his arms darkly sodden and his shirt transparent over his streaming chest. But he had found nothing to eat but grass—grass or the succulent beef of the sun god's cattle.

After another week the rain stopped, but the wind still gusted from the north-west—a gale fit to drive them back the way they had come, back into the mouth of Charybdis and the six jaws of Scylla. Odysseus took his old cockerel, his mascot, and wrung its neck and boiled it in seawater—beak, claws, and all. The stew tasted of sand and sinew, and it was as tough as bridles and sandals and bowstrings. They ate in silence, sheltering under the boat from the clouds of sand that scudded ahead of the wind. Toward the end of the frugal meal, the boat began to rock. It toppled over, and loose oars clattered down on top of the men. They scarcely had the strength to protect themselves. It was not the wind that had blown the boat over: a large cow was scratching its fat hide against the wooden hull.

Forty-five pairs of eyes looked askance at Odysseus. Forty-five hearts brooded. This is a glorious end, they seemed to say, for men who survived the Trojan War.

"I shall go and pray to Athene of the gray eyes and to Great Zeus, father of the gods," said Odysseus sharply. "We were not saved from Charybdis and the six-headed Scylla for the skin to fall off our bones in the company of cows." He walked away slowly; his brains were dizzy and his eyesight smudged with hunger. Some friendly cows fell in behind him and followed him to the other side of the island where, like priests in attendance, they watched Odysseus make his supplication to the gods.

"O Athene! Goddess of War! Can nothing but the flame of battle fire your gray eyes? Is it of no interest to you that your champions in war are jointless with hunger and their bones are hollow and empty of marrow? Was it for this that you strung the taut longbow of my body and armed it with arrows of cunning? The bowstring is frayed almost to breaking, and the arrows have no more strength to fly! Plead my cause in the halls of heaven or distract Poseidon for an hour so that we may creep out from under the shadow of his anger! You alone know what sacrifices I will make to you and to Almighty Zeus if ever I reach Ithaca alive. You whispered in my ear the secret of Circe's potion; you planted the little white moli flower at my feet; you filled Charybdis's gaping mouth with water as we passed by. For what? For us to scatter our shining bones among the sun's cattle? To die among cows?"

A little brown bird fluttered past his head, and, in turning, Odysseus saw the bird light on the bristles of a prickly cactus. And there! In the heart of the cactus was a prickly pear—flame-orange and peppered with black spines. He wrapped his arm in his cloak and reached in for the pear, rubbing off the skin against the ground. It was a miserable fruit: spines still found their way into the roof of his mouth. But to a man who had not eaten for two weeks, except for a mouthful of cockerel broth, it filled him like roast meat and left him with nothing but the longing to sleep. He lay down in the shelter of the cactus. Just as he began to doze, he realized that the wind had changed direction.

He dreamed of making grateful sacrifice to the gods on the shores of Ithaca, and he woke with the savor of it in his nose . . . the savor of roasting beef. The wind had changed, as he had prayed it would. But now it brought on it a smell that choked all happiness in his heart.

Leaping up, arms flailing and sandals slipping, he ran back across the island. The smell grew stronger in his nostrils. The dreadful certainty grew stronger in his heart. He reached the beach in time to see Eurylochus scraping an empty hide with his battle sword. The skinned beef rolled on a spit. The other cows stood round at a distance with large, sad eyes, uncomprehending.

"You fools! You godless fools! We are all dead men!" cried Odysseus picking up Eurylochus by collar and belt and flinging him bodily into the surf. Then he turned on Polites, who was sitting cross-legged in the shingle, his head bent over a fistful of meat. "You! Even you! Why didn't you stop them? Does it taste good, the taste of death? I hope so, because it's the last meal you'll ever eat!"

Polites looked up at him, closing one eye against the brightness of the sky. He spoke quietly. "I know it, Master. But there was truth in what Eurylochus said, for all he's three-parts fool. He said that it was better to die on the ocean, fighting the gods, than to die inch by inch of hunger and be mourned by a herd of cows."

But Eurylochus had changed his tune: "Ach, the sun god will never miss one cow. And if he did, would he begrudge one cow to starving men? If you don't want yours, Captain, we'll eat it for you. There's enough emptiness in my belly for the whole herd!"

Odysseus fell on his knees, groaning, and beat his forehead on the ground. The smoke from the fire and the blackening baron of beef was carried by the wind up into the sky, across the very path of the sinking sun. Into the silence that had fallen over the crew came one mournful bellow. They looked round them, but all the cows had walked off and were out of sight. Their eyes—every man's—came to rest on the smoking carcass roasting on the spit, and the whites of each man's eyes showed in sheerest terror. The carcass bellowed again.

"To sea! To sea!" cried Odysseus, jumping to his feet. "When the sun drives overhead, he'll look down and count his cows. Then he'll melt the brains in your head and the bones in your limbs if you're still here! If we set sail now, we shall have all night before the sun god can take his revenge." Odysseus barely believed his own words, but his men were eager to believe. They carved themselves hunks of cooked meat from the spitted roast, righted the boat, and each man posted his shining oar between its thole-pins. They launched energetically, their strength renewed by the food, their speed redoubled by the danger. Odysseus would not eat one mouthful of the meat, and he boarded the ship with his brain still dizzy, his eyesight still smudged with hunger.

The mast was raised, and the mended sail flowered against its mast-stem. As the Island of Helios dropped below the horizon, the sun god soared over their heads, dazzling bright in his shining chariot, dropping down toward the rosy arch of the sunset. There was a flash of green at the moment he disappeared from sight.

Night fell, and a million stars cascaded, like pebbles hurled down on the unloved, like sparks of white-hot anger. As morning approached, the men grew more and more silent. Only Eurylochus was noisy in his confidence: "We're safe now. The sun god won't trouble himself about one dead cow."

But when the sun rose next morning, there was a ridge of dark cloud above it like a scowling eyebrow over a glaring eye. Sunbeams searched the ocean and lighted on the lonely boat bobbing on the brimming waves, and a wind sprang up in the west that was like a voice calling over the sea: "Poseidon! Poseidon! There is Odysseus!"

The sea writhed. The smooth swell flexed like muscles. The sky lowered, and the sea rose as if it would crush the ship between. Then strings of water, like the stringing saliva in the corners of a mad dog's mouth, joined sea to sky, and waterspouts stood all round: a forest of waterspouts, a colonnade of pillars, as though the surface of the sea were a palace and the sky its roof held up with columns of water. And from down in the sea's cellar, the king of the palace was coming. . . .

Odysseus held the tiller. Polites stood up, although the boat was rolling and pitching. His abandoned oar was tugged out through its slit and floated away as he walked the length of the deck. When he stood face to face with Odysseus, he said, "Farewell, Master. Remember my face when we meet again in the Underworld."

"Farewell, old friend," Odysseus replied, as they

embraced. "I would call your name across the ocean myself, but my voice cracks at the thought of parting from you: the spirits might not hear me."

So Polites faced the heaving ocean and cupped his hands round his mouth and called his own name across the twisting sea lanes: "Polites! Polites! Polites!"

An arching wave as dark as the walls of the Underworld itself reared up over the boat. Beneath them was water, beside them was water, above them was breaking water. Then the wave crashed down on the boat, smashing the mast so that it fell on Eurylochus, instantly killing him. As the wave withdrew, it dragged with it the mast and sail and, tangled in the ropes, the body of drowned Polites.

There! Shoulders of green water ruptured the melting sea and tangled locks of foam shook in the sky. "Let each man call his own name across the ocean!" cried Odysseus into the teeth of the wind, and those who heard him cupped their hands to their mouths and called across the thundering sea:

"Demos!"

"Stavros!"

"Nicoliades!"

"Georgi!"

"Platonis!"

All the shining oars were snapped off short, like the legs of a beetle pulled off by a child. Some of the men were run through with their own sharp-ended oars.

Some were seized from their thwarts by snatching waves. The sea had sixty-thousand jaws, and each as hungry as the mild-mannered Scylla. The wind went about and carried them back past the Island of Helios. The sun god drove his bright chariot to the top of Noonday Hill and poured down molten heat between the tempest clouds. He blistered the skin of the rowers and dried up the marrow in their bones. But then Poseidon, jealous of his revenge, blotted out the sun with pitch-black clouds, so that he might kill Odysseus in the privacy of darkness.

Chapter Nine

An Eternity

"**BREATHE IN, CHARYBDIS,** and swallow down Odysseus and all his hopes!" Poseidon's voice hissed in every spume-frayed wave. The forked lightning of his trident jabbed one prong to the right and two to the left of the hull. The water that broke over the ship was hot now, and the air was full of ash from the fires of the Wandering Rocks. The sea was a bowl where dead fish stewed. And Charybdis was breathing in.

Faster and faster the surface layers of the sea were slipping toward the Hole. The mast of the death ship was still at the center, still stirring the cauldron Charybdis. Some of the remaining crew leaped overboard and tried to swim, seeing that the ship was doomed to be swallowed. The undertow snatched them, sure as sharks, under and down. The rest clung to the lurching boat in the hope that Charybdis would breathe out and halt its whirling for long enough to spare them. But the downward spiral was only just beginning, and Charybdis the Hole grew deeper and whirled faster by the second.

Poseidon's angry breath sped them toward it. All the litter of the sea—splintered spars, the fins of whales, barrels washed overboard, broken breakwaters, rafts of weed, fishing pots, and drowned sailors—washed against the hull with thuds and bangs. Then it was gone, over the glassy rim of Charybdis, and the ship was flung by its speed out over the empty well of the whirlpool, enshrouded in spindrift and spray.

From the aft deck, Odysseus flung himself into the air. His hands clawed over his head. He grabbed the twisted branches of the leafless, salt-blasted fig tree that overhung the abyss of Charybdis. The earth at its roots shifted; pebbles fell away into the swirling water; the branch sagged under the weight of Odysseus. But it held.

Had he not gone hungry for weeks on the Island of Helios, had his thick-set body not been reduced to ribs, pelvis, and wasted shanks, he would have wrenched tree and root out of the cliff and fallen with them into the gaping whirlpool. But he clung, as thin as a grasshopper clinging to the underside of a blade of grass, and beneath him his ship plunged down to destruction.

Joint parted from joint, plank from keel, tiller from stern, hand from broken oar, fingertips from wreckage, prayers from lips, breath from lungs, life from body, as the *Odyssey* and its crew plunged to their doom in Charybdis's dismal abyss. Not one cry climbed through the roaring spray to Odysseus's ears, but the sound of the sea itself was like the screams of a thousand drowning sailors, the wailing of a thousand widows, the breaking of a thousand hearts.

The sun went down, but inside the tent of spray that canopied Charybdis, Odysseus could not tell night from day, evening from morning. Night fell, while a white hail of spray cascaded over him: every breath was like drowning. The thighbones burned in his hip joints; his arms groaned in their sockets; his sinews unwound from his bones, but still he clung to the fig tree. And Charybdis raged beneath him—so steep-sided that pieces of his brightly painted ship were embedded in the glassy spiral of water, like a frieze on the wall of a temple. The Hole was so deep that the seabed itself was dry at the base. There! A dim gleam came from the king's golden breast-plate and the bronze helmet he had worn to dazzle the gods. Quivering in the sand stood the king's sword . . . until water washed over them and clattered them together like tin pots. They did not float; they were lost from sight under the rising water. Charybdis was breathing out!

Slowly, slowly the vortex of the whirlpool grew shallower—as deep as a well, a cave, a trough, a bowl. . . . Fragments of painted wood that had once been a boat as bright as the spring flowers, jostled each other on the boiling eddy. Odysseus let go his grip on the fig tree and fell the short drop into the lava-warmed sea. He grasped the keel of the *Odyssey* as it swirled out of the sway of Charybdis. It was the only fragment of flotsam he recognized from his own boat. Even the death ship they had seen spinning intact for the space of a tide or two was shattered to sodden, black shards.

Lying on his face and paddling with arms that weighed like lead in their sockets, he floated away from those dreadful straits.

For nine days the sun, still hot with anger, raged on his unarmored back. For eight nights the white moon's reflection swam beside him in the sea. Salt whitened his hair and wrinkled his skin until his own wife would have called him an old man. And just as a grape dries and shrivels into a wrinkled raisin, Odysseus's heart shrank inside him; he let drop the last of his youth into the bottomless ocean where nothing lost is ever found again. When the ninth night fell, clouds swallowed all the stars but one, which floated like a shipwrecked sailor in the edgeless, pitch-black sky.

But the world-encircled sea is not without shores.

There! A heap of blackness like the shoulder of some great sea beast stood out hard and shineless against the slick, black ocean and the cloud-soft darkness of the sky. Odysseus was too weary to move his hands, which hung down through the water and were brushed by unseen fish. But the current carried him closer and closer to the dark outline of the island, and soon his dangling fingers touched sand, and the paintless keel of his broken boat rolled him onto his back. He looked up and saw the one last star dimmed by morning, then sleep swallowed him entirely.

When he woke, someone was singing. The song was so sweet that he thought for a moment that the sea had carried him back to the barren roost of the singing Sirens. But when he stirred, he could feel a down quilt under him and a blanket of lamb's wool over him. His eyes were puffed up with salt water, and he could not see, but small, soft hands were stroking his hair and forehead, and a sweet foam of warm honey was trickling past his lips.

He tried to sit up. "I am Odysseus, King of Ithaca and ruler over . . . "

The singing ceased. "I know very well who you are, Odysseus, for you are ruler of more than Ithaca, Cephalonia, and little wooded Zanthe: you are ruler of my heart. And because you have been chosen by an Immortal, you shall be immortal, too."

"Circe? Is it you?"

There was a tinkling of silver as his nurse dropped the spoon. Some of the softness went out of the voice. "Circe? What's that pig farmer to you? Beside her, I'm the daystar beside a candle." A cool cloth wiped his eyes, and he was able to open them. Leaning over him was a woman dressed in green and yellow, like the spring, and her breath smelled of honeysuckle. She leaned across him, and her hair hung round him like a curtain as she covered his face with kisses.

This is a good place, thought Odysseus. It's not Ithaca,

but it is a good place. Besides, I'm weary. I must rest. He said: "Madam, what's your name, and who are your people?"

"My name is Calypso, and this is my island—Ogygia. There is no one here but me—you and me, my love." She crept under the lambskin blanket and dozed in the angle of his arm.

Little by little, the strong longbow of Odysseus's body grew pliable again, restrung with courage and cunning. His thoughts and plans bristled like a quiverful of arrows worn high on his back, and he put out of his mind Poseidon the Tormentor.

But he could not put out of mind Ithaca or his queen or his son . . . or the words of Tiresias about the suitors swarming round his hives. "I must get home as soon as I can," he told Calypso.

But she only shrugged her white shoulders and stroked his brown arms and said, "I have no boat to give you."

Calypso was a nymph, and her house was a sand-carpeted cave hung with wool rugs and scarlet drapery. It looked out on an arcing bay of white sand and mauve water through a paling of aspen and cypress trees. The land was dappled like a leopard with leafy shade, and white-headed grasses, like the manes of horses, tossed in the jasmine-scented air. Passion flowers, white and purple and open-mouthed, entwined the entrance to the cave, and here Calypso had her loom. The warp and weft were as fine as spiders' thread, and her golden shuttle flew as fast as a sharp-nosed yellow hornet—to and fro, to and fro—while she worked.

But after Odysseus came to Ogygia, Calypso rarely spent time weaving at her loom. She trailed like a shadow at Odysseus's heel, and whenever he turned, he found himself beached in her white arms.

Her kisses tasted like the fruit of the lotus tree; they had the power to make a man want more. For a time, Odysseus became a Lotus Eater in Calypso's arms. But as week turned to month and month to year, he tired of her admiration. Whenever he said, "Today I shall go fishing," she replied, "Don't go. I love you. Don't you love me?"

Whenever he said, "Today I shall practice my archery," she replied, "Silly bows and arrows. Don't you love me any more? Stay here with me."

Whenever he said, "I'm getting fat, and my muscles are weakening," she replied, "No matter. I love you as you are."

When he told her stories of Troy, he could not speak three words before she interrupted him with sighs and exclamations: "How wonderful! No wonder I love you!"

Even when he did not speak to her, she would repeat, "I love you, I love you, I love you." It was not conversation as he remembered it. He remembered sitting under his vine-arch with Penelope and discussing affairs of state.

"I don't care about politics," said Calypso. "I only care about you."

He remembered how Penelope had told him stories to while away the winter evenings.

"I don't know any stories," said Calypso. "Besides, you tell stories so much better than I ever could."

He remembered how wise Penelope had been in matters of history, how they had walked along the headlands of Ithaca and imagined how the world had looked when no one but the gods played on its open places.

"Why look to the past?" said Calypso when he told her. "The present is all that matters—that and our future together—you and me forever and ever and ever."

He remembered how, as they had walked on those summer evenings, Penelope had pointed out all the little flowers to him, naming them by name and making up poetry about the birds and the sea. "I want to walk over the headland, Calypso," he said.

"Walk? Why walk when we can lie down and kiss? How can I kiss you when you keep talking so?"

Odysseus gave a sudden groan and hurried out of the cave. He walked and walked, while there was light left to see by, and then he sat down on a cliff overlooking the sea and wept bitterly, his knees pressed into the sockets of his eyes and his body rocking—to and fro, to and fro.

"Oh, Penelope! Penelope! What will become of you and your son, with me a prisoner on this mound of sugar? O you gods, who sent me here to eat syrup off a poisoned spoon—remember me! Remember me! Remember me!"

"Have you forgotten?" said Queen Penelope to the suitor Eurymachus. "I am a married woman, and my husband, whose food you are eating, is Odysseus, hero of Troy."

Eurymachus wiped his mouth on his hand and grinned at her. "Forgotten, Lady? Forgotten great Odysseus? Of course not! He's the hero who drowned on his way back from Troy and left a widow and no one to rule over Ithaca."

White-faced, Penelope plucked at the weft of her loom with nervous rage. "No one to rule? He left his son, didn't he? He left Telemachus! He'll come home soon with news of his father, or perhaps with Odysseus himself."

Eurymachus stood up. "No, Lady. I told you, and you knew already in your heart of hearts, that your worthy husband died long since. What? He could have walked barefoot from Troy across the seabed by now, if he was still alive. Choose a new husband. Look! There are plenty to choose from here in your own palace! Take a young, handsome husband who'll give you some fun in the years to come. Your boy, Telemachus, may have fallen into the hands of pirates or been swallowed in the sea like his father. Or maybe he's fallen in love with some pretty face a thousand miles away. And if he returns? What then? He's only a boy—years from manhood. How could he hope to hold the island states of Ithaca against . . .

against those who would take them from him? Your palace is charming. Your food is excellent. But all this waiting about . . . it gets on a man's nerves. I strongly advise you to choose one of us for a husband, before anyone unmannerly thinks of helping himself to the crown."

"Are you threatening me, Eurymachus?" whispered Penelope, trembling so with fury that she dropped the shuttle of her loom.

"Me, Madam? Your devoted admirer and slave? Your ardent lover whose very heart waits on your permission to beat? Me, threaten you? Never!"

"Then, if you are my slave, tell this to the other suitors and pay heed to it yourself. On this loom I'll weave a wedding veil. When it's finished, I'll wear it in marriage to one of you. Then Ithaca will have a king again. Tell them, will you, Eurymachus?"

"Lady! Beloved Penelope! I myself will fetch you a veil woven by fifty maidens out of cobweb if that's all that's keeping you from marrying!"

But she held up her hand and succeeded in smiling with all sweetness. "You ask me to admit that my dear Odysseus is dead. Very well. Give me this little while to mourn for him while I weave. It's only fair, Eurymachus."

The suitor bowed with a great show of respect, but behind his hand he was grinning, for he believed he would not have long to wait before the crown of Ithaca was his. Outside the room, he caught the sleeve of

Antinous, another of the suitors, and led him aside into a dark corner. "The old girl is weakening. She's weaving a bit of lace, and when it's done she'll marry. Now, about Telemachus. If he gets any older, he'll start thinking of himself as heir to the crown. I think it would be kinder if we let him know the true situation—keep him from raising his hopes unduly. Don't you agree?"

"I see what you mean," said Antinous.

"Let's take a few men out to Asteris, to meet him on his homeward voyage. Ships always put in there for the last night. Then we can . . . discuss things with him."

"Slit his throat, you mean?"

"Antinous, you're so crude sometimes," sighed Eurymachus. "Yes, slit his throat."

When the suitors heard the news that Penelope would marry when her veil was woven, they hacked open a particularly large barrel of wine from the cellars of Pelicata Palace. Then they drank themselves merry and stumbled upstairs to the room where Penelope's loom stood in the daylight of the window. They stood round and watched her shoot the shining shuttle—to and fro, to and fro.

"Be done in no time," they whispered.

"A month at most."

"Let's take bets on how long she takes—I've got a better idea! Let's take bets on who she chooses. Ha-ha-ha!"

Later, much later that night, when the suitors were all asleep with Pelicata wine on their chins and their dirty sandals under Pelicata's white blankets, Penelope got up from her royal bed. She crept along the corridors, past the tall gray squares of window and the view of the moon-silver sea, to the room where her loom stood. In her hand was a pair of scissors. Stitch by stitch, she undid everything she had woven that day.

"This veil of mine shall be longer in the making than all the reefs of the sea built up from the tiny lives of shellfish. It won't be finished before Telemachus comes back. It won't be finished before my hair is as white as salt and my skin as wrinkled as the sea. It won't be finished before my dear Odysseus comes home—even though he doesn't come and doesn't come and doesn't ever come. O you gods! Have you lived so long up there in the cold, thin air of Olympus that your hearts have died within you? Or have you forgotten what it is to be in love?"

Chapter Ten

The Quarrelsome Gods

IN THE EAST, the sun gleamed on the greening copper domes and palaces of princes in barren, stony kingdoms. In the west, the sun was just rising on shivering barbarians blue with cold. In the north, dark-haired gypsies were still sleeping where they had fallen down with weariness from dancing under the moon. And to the south, the sunlight caught on the golden shuttle of Calypso the nymph as it flew—to and fro, to and fro—across her loom. From the far side of her island, smoke was rising from a sacrificial fire.

From the highest terraces of Mount Olympus, the gods could see every mortal and lowly Immortal under the sun. The goddess Athene stood on one such terrace and sniffed up the sweet sandalwood fragrance of Odysseus's fire. Round her the lazy gods sprawled in ones and twos on silver cushions lined with cloud. Their late sleeping irritated her. The perfection of their line-free, eggshell-smooth faces irritated her. The heady scent of roses irritated her. Tipping her warrior helmet back on her head, she banged the base of her silver spear on the ground.

"You're vexed," said Hermes. He lay on his back on a couch, his hands under his head and his blue cover slipping onto the floor. "What do you see that vexes you so much when you look over there?"

"I see a good man making sacrifice, and his smoke pouring past the gods' nostrils without raising so much as a sneeze! Does religious devotion count for nothing anymore?"

Hermes lazily lifted his head. "Ah. You mean Odysseus. You always liked these hairy-faced mortals with their black-wool arms. He puts me in mind of a sheep—all that wool and bleating."

"He's been held captive on that island for seven years now, weeping and breaking his heart, and what do we do to help him?"

"Held captive? On Ogygia? With Calypso? That's one prison where most men would pay to be penned up. I call it most ungrateful of Odysseus to spend all his time beating his head on the floor and weeping. Worse things happen at sea, so they say!" Hermes laughed and wagged his heels in the air. "Your trouble is, you're jealous!"

"Jealous? Of her?" The goddess of gray eyes tossed her head, threw back her shoulders, and strode purposefully into the hall of heaven. She had determined to speak to Zeus while his mind was uncluttered. Already prayers had begun to rise up on the thermals of morning air; soon the prayers of worshipers from all over the sea-encircling world would be racketing about the quiet corridors of Olympus. And Zeus would find it all too easy to brush aside her request.

"Zeus! Father! Mighty father of all the gods," she began briskly as she entered the blue marble hall. Her sandals slapped the ethereal pavement. "Has Poseidon's foul temper poisoned all heaven that we no longer show mercy to a faithful worshiper—a man who makes sacrifices every day and libations of salt-water tears? Is a lowly sea nymph to be allowed to imprison one of my champions—one of those I crowned with fame on the Trojan battlefields?"

The father of the gods sat among the swathes of his train, which creased and interfolded like the foothills of the Pindus Mountains, topped by the snowy whiteness of his hair. He had a young man's face, but his eyes were as old as the lakes that sit in the remote craters of extinct volcanoes. "We all know your feelings, child Athene, on the subject of Odysseus."

"Feelings?" Athene bridled, her nostrils flaring beneath her gray eyes. "I am the goddess of war! My feelings are those of a commander who sees one of his men mistreated!"

"Yes, yes. Of course. Naturally. But warrior Odysseus did blind Polyphemus, son of Poseidon. And his men did eat one of the cattle of Helios—the sun god's pride and joy. Must they have no revenge?"

"Is seven years not punishment enough?" retorted Athene. "Polyphemus broke all laws of hospitality and ate Greeks like apples and spat out their souls like pips. No beef passed Odysseus's lips, and the guilty men are washing about in the cold sea, with dogfish gnawing on their bones. Is seven years' imprisonment in the cave of Calypso not punishment enough for any mortal? The years Odysseus has lost will never come again."

"Imprisonment? On Ogygia? That's one prison where most men would pay to be penned up. And I hear tell that Calypso has offered Odysseus eternal life if he will love her in return," said Zeus in slow, measured words.

A frisson of anger shook Athene from head to foot. The base of her spear cracked against the celestial pavement so that hail fell onto the places beneath. "That meddlesome strumpet! That presumptuous nymph! If we are going to let her make gods of all her lovers, heaven will soon be full to overflowing. Are we to jostle shoulder to shoulder through eternity with mortals trooping continually up to Olympus's gates saying, 'Calypso sent me' and 'Calypso made me immortal. Let me in!'?"

"Enough!" Zeus held up his hand. The smallest contracting of his brows sent thunder rolling round the horizon. Athene's words froze on her lips in awe. But her bold eyes still rested on the father of the gods. He said, "It has been in my mind for some time to let Odysseus leave Ogygia. It pleases me that he has rejected Calypso's offer of immortality. Besides, his wife's prayers rise up on every puff of wind, and his son's, too. The name Odysseus seems never to be out of my head. For the sake of my peace, I will send Hermes to command Calypso to let him go. . . . But since he is mortal, he must use mortal means to reach Ithaca's shores. No galleys of cloud. No rainbow bridges. No silver dolphins to carry him over the waves. Only a wooden raft made with his own hands. And one of the gods must keep old Poseidon busy with talk and his back turned, because I won't forbid the old Sea-Shaker his revenge."

"But why, Father Zeus? Why? Why? Why?"

"Because, my daughter, I look at you and I ask myself how I would feel if some small, braggartly mortal put out your two gray eyes with a white-hot stake of wood."

Hermes strapped on his golden sandals—the ones with wings at their heels—and leaped over the parapet of heaven to begin his downward flight. Men looking up thought that they glimpsed a sea eagle stooping over the fish-silver ocean: the sight was too bright for mortal eyes to see his golden cap and plaited rod of serpents.

He landed outside the cave mouth of Ogygia's nymph, beside her loom. It stood abandoned, the shuttle hanging down by a gossamer thread. Inside the cave, Calypso's voice was loud and shrill: "I tell you, you shan't! Must you be forever asking? You shan't go. I love you—and in time you'll learn to love me. What, more tears? There'd be tears enough if you had to change me for old Penelope. It's twenty years since you saw her. Don't you realize how age twists a mortal woman's face and melts her figure into a shapeless—"

There was a sharp crack. Calypso came running to the mouth of the cave with the red shape of a hand burning on her cheek. She was startled to see Hermes, who stood quietly listening, with a look of amusement on his face.

"What do you want?" she snapped.

"I have a message for you from Great Zeus, father of all the gods. . . . You have to let him go."

Calypso grew still paler, and the mark on her cheek grew brighter in contrast. "Is this your doing, Hermes? Can't you bear to see one of the Immortals in love with a mortal man?"

Hermes spread his hands with a look of injured innocence. "I'm just a messenger. This is a command from Zeus."

"It's her doing. It's Athene's doing. She's jealous of me. That's what it is. Well, I won't let him go. I won't! She shan't have him. He's mine!"

"Calypso! It would seem he's nobody's, this warrior sea captain with the shaggy arms. No one owns his heart—unless it's his queen Penelope and the island he's pined for these last seven years. Seven years, and he hasn't learned to love you yet. Is he so slow to learn, this man whose cunning is likened to the arrows from a bow?"

"Yes!" cried Calypso, furiously rubbing her cheek.

"Yes, he's stupid and obstinate. He wants nothing but to build a raft and put to sea."

"Then give him an iron ax and tell him which trees he may cut down. Find him rope and a sail and then cast your eyes over the ocean for a new lover."

Calypso took up the shuttle and jabbed it angrily into the weave of her tapestry—a tapestry picturing a man dressed in a golden breastplate and a plumed helmet of bronze with a long and shining nosepiece. She said bitterly, "You idle Olympians. You have nothing to do but look over the parapet of heaven and make mischief. In time he would have loved me. I know it."

Hermes kicked up his winged heels and sprang into the air. Men looking up thought they saw an albatross riding on the thermal columns of air as he spiraled into the sky. But he did not fly back to Mount Olympus. He flew from atoll to atoll, using the islands like stepping stones. At last he sighted a brightly painted ship trailing behind it a wake of white water. He dropped down, down to the pitching deck of Telemachus's boat. Men looking up thought they saw a gull stoop on a fish. But Telemachus looked over his shoulder and found the dark, Levantine face of a sailor close to his. A heavy brown hand rested on his shoulder. Hermes had disguised himself as the ship's first mate.

"Shall we be mooring at Asteris on this voyage?" the mate enquired.

"I shall moor there tonight," said Telemachus. "It has a deep-water bay in the north . . . perfectly placed, and there's fresh water. People who sail from Samos to Ithaca always moor there on the last stretch of the voyage. It's only a day from Ithaca, and the water is always running low on board by the time we reach it. . . . "

The Levantine nodded and said, "Just so. Hmm. May I make a suggestion, Captain . . . ?"

Eurymachus and Antinous, those murderous schemers, dropped anchor in the northernmost bay of Asteris. Spiny with swords and bristling with arrows, they and a band of suitors thirty-strong rowed ashore. Some hid by the spring; some watched from the promontories; some dug a deep pit and lined it with thornbushes and covered it with leaves; some ranged themselves, bows strung, round the pretty, sheltered bay. Their ship was moored out of sight. No one arriving from the sea would see that others were already there, lying in ambush. Pots of oil stood ready to light when the moment came, so that the archers could shoot flying flame into the sails of Telemachus's ship. Whether by knife, sword, arrow, fire, or drowning, Telemachus must surely die.

Only one fear remained in Antinous's mind. "Supposing he has found his father. Supposing we snare the bull as well as the calf in our trap?"

"What? After twenty years? The man's dead. When I said it the first time, I didn't know or care if it was true.

But after all this time, the man's dead for sure. And if he's not dead, he's forty years old, which is as good as dead. Do you expect me to tremble at the thought of a grizzle-bearded forty-year-old and his beardless son? If they both come, we'll kill them both. Right? Of course, right. The only chore is the waiting."

There! As the sun declined, and evening light poured thick as honey through the sea lanes and dry-land pathways, a brightly painted boat came into sight. The murderers crouched low in their places. They wore no piece of metal for the sun to glint on. They had blackened their faces with mud, for fear Telemachus would glimpse them among the bushes and suspect an ambush. They lay perfectly still, testing the sharpness of their knives against their thumbs, laying arrows across their bows. In a minute or two, Telemachus would sail into the arms of the bay and drop anchor for the night—drop anchor forever. And from overhead a hail of arrows would hurtle onto him and fill him as full of spines as a hedgehog. Then he would roast beneath his own canvas when it fell, burning, from the mast.

Eurymachus licked his lips, which were dry with excitement. Afterward he would hurry home and break the sad news gently to the queen that Telemachus had died in a storm at sea. Ah, how comforting he would be! When the veil was finished and the grieving queen was ready to marry, she would surely choose the suitor who had comforted her in her hour of grief. . . .

The brightly painted ship was only a furlong from the island—almost within range. Antinous eased his arrow on its bowstring. He would hit Telemachus right between his foolishly wide, blue eyes.

A cry came over the water—Telemachus calling instructions to his crew. "Raise the genoa and lean on your oars, men! There's plenty of water to drink in Ithaca and wine to go with it. We'll row all night with this fair wind." And the brightly painted boat skirted the island of Asteris and did not drop anchor in the pretty, sheltered bay.

Antinous gave a great groan of dismay and stood up to watch the ship skim out of sight. Then he cursed foully and smashed his bow across his knee in a fit of rage.

Odysseus felled twenty trees and split the trunks lengthwise. He roped them together and bored a hole to take the tall mast. All the while he worked, Calypso said nothing, but sat, chin in hands, with pouting lips and a frown between her eyes. But on the last day, when he had finished, she moved away up the beach, scuffing her heels, and returned with a tapestry folded over her arm.

"This may do for a sail," she said. "But it has no magic power."

"Yes, it has!" cried Odysseus, kissing her. "It has the power to encourage me! Thank you, Calypso!" The tapestry was of a cockerel, its head thrown back and its wings spread in crowing. Odysseus tacked it to the crosstree where it tugged and cracked in the breeze. He rigged a tiller from a forked branch and the keel of his broken ship and built a wattle fence round the edge of the raft to keep it from being swamped. The nymph gave him food and drink for the journey, and for the first time in many years, she seemed a most agreeable companion. He was even prepared to kiss her once more when the time came to say good-bye.

The tapestry cockerel swelled its breast as the sail filled with wind. The imprints made in the sand by the heavy logs filled with salt water, like eyes filling with tears, as the raft was set afloat by successive waves. The tiller oar cut one white wound in the dark water beyond the creamy surf.

And Calypso stood on the white sand with one hand waving, the golden shuttle in her fingers as though she were weaving magic in the salty air. She did not return to her loom at the cave mouth until the cockerel sail of Odysseus's raft was crossing the horizon and the figure of Odysseus was lost from sight.

The raft made good progress while the sea was flat. It twisted and rolled when the sea grew choppy, slapping the waves down and jarring Odysseus's knees. When the sun god drove his flaming chariot up to Noonday Hill and across the sky, Odysseus rigged a canopy to keep off the scorching heat and in case the god looked down and recognized him. But it was not the sun god who first recognized Odysseus.

It was Poseidon.

Slung in a hammock of cloud between the north and easterly horizons, Poseidon the Earth-Shaker and Sea-Shifter rolled over . . . and saw a speck of wood floating on the ocean. He might have taken it for flotsam from some shipwreck, but for the brightly woven sail flapping over it. Poseidon narrowed his eyes, to see better against the brightness of the water. His brows, purple as thunderclouds, puckered, and his nostrils flared. "ODYSSEUS!"

He summoned up, from the northern realms of the white sea, all the white horses of his herds and, with whip-cracks of thunder, stampeded them over the wave-tussocked meadow of the sea.

Odysseus looked over his shoulder and saw the dark clouds rise up on the horizon, as dust clouds rise up from under the hoofs of galloping horses. He saw a mass of whiteness and heard the thunder of hoofs. He just had time to drop his sail before he saw the manes of spray, the curved necks of over-arching waves, the pounding hoofs of gray water that dropped in gouts out of the over-arching waves, and the whiplash thunderbolts driving on the stampede. He wrapped his arms round the mast as a child wraps its arms round its mother's knees.

Poseidon's horses pounded over the raft—great waves foaming at the mouth, sweating foam, and snorting foam out of black nostrils. Their watery hoofs splintered the beams of Odysseus's floor and broke the rope so that the floor opened and sea rushed in between the logs. Then it was sucked back down again, and with it went Odysseus, through the boards of his raft and into the dark shock of the cold sea. When he surfaced, the raft had already been swept far away from him, a heap of firewood loosely lashed together with tangled ropes. The sail slipped to the bottom of the sea where undulating skates and manta rays swam over it, wondering.

Like a Laestrygonian, Poseidon fished for Odysseus with his trident, jabbing with pronged lightning: one prong to the right of him, two prongs to the left. The sea and sky turned black with bruising. But Odysseus swam with the speed of a darting fish after his raft, clung to it, and got his legs astride a single log and slumped facedown, like a baron of meat on a spit. The rain drummed on his back until he thought it would beat him senseless. Huge dark shapes seemed to swim up from the depths in front of his exhausted eyes, and he thought they must be mountainous sea creatures of the kind that sip shipwrecked sailors off the surface of the sea. At any moment a guzzling mouth might bite off his arms or legs as they dangled down through the water. . . .

There! Something took firm grip of his thigh and almost pulled him off the log. A fishy tail writhed past his head. "O goddess Athene! Why did you not let me die in Troy and have my armor shared out between the heroes and my name shared out among the world's storytellers? That it should be like this!—to have my body shared out between the fishes and my name swallowed by sea beasts. . . . " He tried to call his name over the ocean for the ghosts to hear in the Underworld. But seawater filled his mouth and half drowned him.

"Why call your name? I already know who you are, Odysseus, King of Ithaca. My name is Ido."

He turned his head, and there, her hands round his thigh, was a sea nymph, flicking the silvery green scales of her tail, her hair spreading on the water round her sweet face, like the leaves round a water lily. "Take this scarf, Odysseus, and tie it round your chest. Then swim for land—over there. I and the other sea nymphs have been watching your game with Poseidon. It's most exciting. I'm so glad you've left Ogygia and started to play again. I shouldn't help you, I suppose, but Poseidon is always winning. It's tiresome to see him winning all the time. And truly he's not half as pleasing to look at as you, Odysseus. The other nymphs will be angry with me, but one little cheat—one little helping hand—how can it change the outcome of the game so very much? You're still so many miles from Ithaca. . . . "

She gave a playful tug on his leg, which overbalanced the log and spilled Odysseus into the sea, before she thrashed her tail and dived back down through the seething sea. His leather skirt began to pull him under. He unfastened it and let it drop, kicked off his long-stringed sandals, and tied the sea nymph's scarf round his chest. It buoyed him up, and from the crest of a wave that threw him bodily into the air, he glimpsed the Land of Scheria.

Its coast was as jagged as though when the gods shaped the mainland with axes, this shard had flown up from their axes and wedged itself in the flesh of the sea. Jagged pinnacles lay offshore from jagged precipices— the rock so sharp that even the sea birds lighting there screamed at the sharpness. There was no beach, no bay, no harbor, no haven. Poseidon's mares hurled themselves against the cliffs and shattered into glittering walls of spray. But however many spent themselves on Scheria's shredding shore, there were always more let loose from the paddock sky to trample Odysseus and tumble him on toward the rocks.

Chapter Eleven

The Stone Ship

THOUGH THE WINDOWS of Pelicata Palace looked out on three separate bays, and into each came the striped sea, always arriving, wave after wave, and though Penelope looked out every day as she sat at her loom weaving, Odysseus did not come and did not come and did not ever come. The harbor now was crowded with little boats as, with every tide, new suitors arrived to tempt her with their looks, their worthless presents, or with flattery. But only one boat newly arrived in the harbor gave her any joy. Her son, Telemachus, had returned from searching for his father.

There he stood in the doorway, the shine of sun in his hair and sea salt on his skin. "Well? What news?" said Penelope, hardly breathing as she spoke. "Is he alive? Is he coming? Has he forgotten us? Or have the gods forgotten all of us?"

Telemachus laid down his spear and sword and kissed his mother gently. "I sailed to the northern shores of the ocean to Pylos, Nestor's home. Nestor fought alongside Father under the walls of Troy. I asked him if he had seen a shipwreck or heard of any accident."

"And what did he tell you? Good news? Bad news?"

"No news at all. Nestor helped Odysseus set sail from the shores of Troy: twelve Ithacan boats he helped to carry into the sea. They put to sea together, then struck off in different directions, lost sight of each other by nightfall, lost the sound of each other's oars before morning."

Then Penelope's heart sank like a little boat.

"But listen, Mother! He's heard no bad news—no news of shipwrecks or pirates or wars. He told me to visit old Menelaus, who set sail that same day. So I traveled by chariot and horse, by donkey and by foot, across great dry seas of rocks and dust to Lacedaemon, to King Menelaus's palace."

Penelope was impatient to know. "What did he tell you? Good news? Bad news?"

"No news at all."

Penelope's heart sank like a little pebble.

"But, Mother! He told us not to give up hope. He traveled for years himself to reach home. He was ship-wrecked in Egypt—Egypt, Mother!—on the southern shores of the world! But there he was, after all his troubles, alive and well and home. I'm certain my father is alive. And one day soon he will come home. The strangest thing happened as I sailed past Asteris. . . . "

But his mother had turned and was looking out of her

window toward the waves, arriving, always arriving, always beaching on the shores of Ithaca. "I'm sure, too, Telemachus. I'm sure that everything they said is true. But how long must I creep barefoot through my own halls night after night to unpick my weaving and save myself from marriage to one of these . . . these vermin? And when they've eaten every sheep, drunk every tun of wine, torn every blanket, and sold every brick of the royal palace, will he be grateful for what I've done? What kind of king will he be when this scum has frittered away his kingdom?"

Odysseus was hurled up against a rocky pinnacle like a prisoner thrown into a pit of spears to be pierced through and through. He wrapped his arms and legs round it as he had clung to the mast of his raft, and Poseidon's mares galloped over him. And as each wave retreated, it tried to drag him away from his handhold, filling his nose with water, prying at his fingers, tearing at his shirt. He would willingly have let go: the rocks were razor sharp and covered in grazing barnacles. But then the sea would only have hurled him against the cliff. When dark green, slimy weeds caught round his legs and flapped, he thought it was his skin flapping from the bone. Scum creamed in his hair. He looked to right and left, but the cliffs seemed unbroken for as far as he could see.

There! A streak of lighter blue in the ocean showed

where a narrow river was issuing out to sea to the east, mixing its fresh water with the brine. He put his bare feet to the pinnacle of rock and launched himself in the direction of the estuary. The sea shouldered him up against the cliff, but, little by little, he edged his painful way toward the tiny estuary.

He swam against the current. He put down his feet and walked over mussels and limpets until he was wading in fresh river water—though all the time the river tried to push him back out to sea. Climbing out onto the bank was like climbing Olympus itself to the weary Odysseus. He crawled into the cradle of a split olive tree that overhung the river and went to sleep still crouched on hands and knees.

He woke to the sound of voices so high and melodic that he thought they must belong to nymphs. Wrapped in anguish, he lay as still as a dead man and prayed. "O fearsome Athene, goddess of the battlefield, whose only thoughts are of duty and war and manliness, forbid that yet another nymph should take a liking to me! If one more Immortal falls in love with me, I think I'll hurl myself off this island's cliffs and let Poseidon use me as he pleases!" Then he parted the leaves of the olive tree and said, loudly, "I'm a married man and I have no time to spend in loving you!"

There was a squeak of surprise, and five young maidens hid themselves up to their shoulders in the river where they had been bathing. Their clothes hung like blossoms on the bushes all round, and the laundry they had brought down to the river floated downstream out of their startled hands. The tallest of the maidens recovered herself and said, "I should think not, sir! I am a princess shortly to be married and I can well do without you, you ragamuffin!"

A sorry-looking hero lowered himself painfully out of the tree—his skirt and sandals gone, his arms and legs etched with gashes, his beard white with salt, and his eyes a fearful red with salt water. When he saw his reflection in the river, he was ashamed to admit that no immortal nymph would have looked at him and sighed. "I am Odysseus, King of Ithaca. My apologies and compliments, Lady, but can you spare me a bite of bread?"

"Not until you turn your back and spare our blushes," said the tallest maiden. "But your sufferings, which must have been many, make you welcome on Scheria. On behalf of my father, King Alcinous, I greet you—whoever you are."

They carried Odysseus back to the palace hidden beneath the laundry. "Because it would hardly be fitting for unmarried maidens to be seen in the company of such a . . . masculine man," explained the Princess Nausicaa, covering up his head with a damp sheet. "Especially a gentleman without skirt or sandals."

The creaking and jiggling of the cart rocked Odysseus to sleep again, and when he woke, the princess and her maidens-in-waiting were nowhere to be seen. He was all alone in the laundry cart, in the yard of King Alcinous's palace. Out of respect for the ladies' good name, he presented himself at the door of the palace as if he had walked all the way from the shore by his own efforts.

The king greeted him hospitably enough and was sympathetic at the news of his shipwreck in the storm. But when Odysseus gave his name, the king threw up his hands in amazement. He called for a feast to be prepared at once and summoned dancers, men and women, to dance in celebration. "Praise be to the gods on Olympus that I should be given the honor of meeting you—and of helping you to a new boat! The stories of your part in the siege of Troy are known all over the world! A day's journey in one of my fast boats will bring you to Ithaca. But tell me, what voyage have you been on that has brought you to my ragged little island?"

Odysseus was startled. "Why, I'm still sailing home from Troy, by way of death and disaster!"

"From Troy? From the Trojan Wars? You can't mean that for ten years and more you've been traveling without ever arriving? Have you been pining in some dungeon or tied to some Moorish oar for a galley slave? What became of the men in your company—the other men of Ithaca?"

Odysseus had just lifted from the bronze plate in front of him a succulent breast of chicken. Suddenly, as his eyes met King Alcinous's eyes, he remembered the

deaths and disasters of his long journey and found he could not eat one bite. His throat was full of tears, as a pipe clogs with leaves when the autumn rains pour down it. He swallowed awkwardly and began the story of his voyage.

When he began, night was falling and the light poured thick as honey along the sea lanes and dry-land pathways. When he finished, night's million stars were cascading into a pale pool of morning near the horizon. All night, as he spoke, an old man sat in a corner and wrote. He had no need of daylight, firelight, moonlight, or the morning's plaited beams, for he was blind. But he cut single words with his right hand in a tablet of wax and read them over with his left.

As Odysseus told his story, it was as if each man listening saw for himself the cruel monsters, the crawling sea, the spiteful gods, the beckoning islands. For a long while after, no one spoke.

Then King Alcinous cleared his throat. "Odysseus, you've seen more on your travels than most men have even heard tell. You've suffered more than most men could bear without their hearts and bodies breaking. But your troubles are over now. Just beyond the horizon, Ithaca lies waiting for you. I'll give you treasure enough to return home in glory, and a boat and crew to carry you there. Now, here's food and drink to give you strength for the journey. And let's pray that at last the gods will give you safe passage home."

Bronze and gold cauldrons, chests of linen, and casks of wine were loaded aboard the finest, fastest ship in the king's fleet. On the far shore of Scheria, there was a large harbor crammed with brightly painted, tall-prowed, tall, proud boats. The island's counselors and statesmen feasted with Odysseus all day long. Their kindness and generosity were worthy of King Aeolus, but their friendship was more gentle and forgiving. Kind as they were, Odysseus could not help but glance at the dawdling sun, hour by hour, and long for sunset when he could set sail across the last stretch of ocean for Ithaca.

When the crew took their places at the oars, Odysseus curled up on the after-deck, on the mound of kingly clothing given him by Princess Nausicaa. He was asleep before the long, polished oars had slit the first white wounds in the creamy ocean.

For week upon month upon year, Odysseus the warrior, whose body was strung like a longbow and whose mind was as quick as arrows, had snatched sleep from between battles, from amidst adventures, and from under the shadow of danger or misery. Even on Calypso's isle, during seven years of idleness, he had slept as a horse sleeps, on its feet, an eyelid's blink away from waking, waiting for the unwelcome touch of Calypso's magical hands. But now he slept so soundly, so profoundly, that the tremors of an earthquake, the caresses of the Scylla, or the crash of a thunderbolt could not have made him stir.

But down in the pit of the ocean's stomach, the Earth-Shaker, the Sea-Shifter, the Earthquake-Maker seethed with anger. Poseidon saw the Scherian ship and in it, Odysseus. And the sea god reared up so high that he pushed his blue-green face through the clouds of Olympus and bawled, "Zeus! Father of the gods! I'm shamed forever! The Scherians have made a laughing stock of me!"

"Calmly, brother! Calmly!" said all-powerful Zeus. "Nobody is laughing at you, nor ever will. Who would dare?"

"Then why is Odysseus sailing home to Ithaca with more treasure under him than he ever looted from Troy? Why are the Scherians helping the man who blinded my son? They're flouting my authority! They're aiding my enemy! They're thwarting my revenge!"

Now Zeus, who had long since formed a fondness for the daring, roguish Odysseus, drew back the clouds and glimpsed an early-morning cove on Ithaca where the waves broke in gentle diagonals over the pebbles. The Scherians rowing ashore leaned so hard on their polished oars that the elegant ship ploughed up the beach and left only its rudder afloat in the surf. Odysseus was ashore, safe from Poseidon's spite.

Even the beaching did not wake him, and the crew carried him—after-deck, linens, and all—and laid him in the shade of an early-morning tree, surrounded by the presents of gold, bronze, and wine. Then they pushed their fast boat back into deep water and climbed aboard.

But Zeus's all-seeing eyes were set so wide apart that he saw, at the selfsame time, Polyphemus, the sea god's son, sitting weeping from his one blind eye. And Zeus pitied the pitiless Poseidon. "What is it you want to do?"

Poseidon's black hair seethed, and his anger frothed at his lips. "I mean to blast that Scherian ship and to shovel a mountain out of the sea to wall up Scheria!" He scowled and hunched his shoulders from which the tides swung. "Will you stop me? Will you let these miserable mortals fly in the face of a god? Since Time began I've hemmed them in—these islands, these island-dwellers. Night and morning they've had me to thank for their wretched lives. Will you let them crawl as they like over my rippling back and forbid me to crush them?"

"Poseidon! Brother!" cried Zeus. "These thankless Scherians have forgotten the honor and respect they owe you. Make an example of them. Why not? Then every mortal who crawls upon the muscles of your rippling back will say, 'Dare I anger Poseidon? No! Look what happened to the Scherian ship!' There is no need to weary yourself walling up Scheria."

Poseidon was startled into silence. Swinging his cloak of tides across his face, he strode and waded round his maze of islands. And finding the Scherian ship at the harbor mouth of Scheria, he clutched it in both hands.

In the space of an oar's beat, the hull was fastened to the bed of the sea with a stem of granite, and the waves broke against it, and the sea birds settled on it, crying.

The planks and the keel, the rudder and its tiller, the mast and its crossbeam, the decks and their hatches, the Scherians and their oars were all turned to stone.

The faces of people who stood on the harbor wall turned rock-gray with fright. They ran to King Alcinous with the terrible news.

"We have offended Poseidon," said the gentle, devout king. "Kill twelve oxen and let's offer them up as a sacrifice to him. . . . But afterward, count the faces aboard the stone ship and tell me if Odysseus, too, is turned to stone."

"He is not, Father," said Nausicaa. "The after-deck, the kingly clothing, and all the presents of gold and bronze are gone. Odysseus is safe on Ithaca."

King Alcinous nodded slowly and gave a sad smile. "Home, yes. But safe? For every friend who laughs with joy to see him, a dozen envious villains will wish he had died in Troy or on the voyage home!"

On the night that Odysseus told his story to King Alcinous and his court, Queen Penelope went to bed early in Pelicata Palace. She left the suitors to drink themselves drunk by her husband's hearth and went to bed. But she did not sleep, for there was the veil to be unwoven, the sewing of the day to be unpicked. When the house fell silent, she wrapped a shawl round her shoulders and crept barefoot to the room where her loom stood in the window.

Though there was no starlight, she moved quickly. She was accustomed to finding her way round bench and table in the dark, to where the rug edges might trip her, to where a careless step might set the fire-irons clattering. Her bare feet knew the way: she held the scissors in her right hand.

Suddenly her shins collided with something soft and warm that grunted, then rolled away. Against the gray square of the window, a man's shape rose up from the floor. "So-ho! Polybus, fetch a lamp! We were right about our little spider. She was only weaving her web to catch out us poor men!"

A light flared up and cast wildly flickering shadows into the eye sockets and cheeks of Eurymachus. He took the scissors out of her hand. "Shame on you, Madam. And all this time I took you for an honorable lady."

There was wine spilled on the floor. Eurymachus and Polybus had fallen asleep drunk in front of the loom, trying to fathom out why the veil never seemed to grow. By accident they had found her out. Now their grinning teeth showed yellow in the lamplight. "The waiting's over, dear lady. The time has come for you to make a choice. Why not choose me, eh? Then I'd never tell the others how Odysseus's grand queen crept in her nightclothes to trick her way out of a bargain."

Penelope drew herself up to her full height, like a swan stretching its wings. "Should I be ashamed, then, of loving my husband too dearly?"

"Twenty years, Lady! That's how long your dear husband's been gone! No one can accuse you of being hasty if you remarry now! But will you keep to your bargain, now you've been caught out in it? Veil or no veil, it's time you were a bride again." And he stood close up against her, menacing, with triumphant eyes gleaming down into her face.

"How am I to choose? So many men, all of equal merit," said Penelope bitterly.

"That's for you to decide, Lady. But tomorrow. You must decide tomorrow. Choose looks or charm or wealth . . . but choose."

Chapter Twelve

A Stranger at the Door

WHEN ODYSSEUS FINALLY woke, he could not think where he was. At first he thought it was Ogygia where, in seven years, he had slept away nights on many different beaches, with never an eye to their shape or features. Then he remembered the raft and thought he must have drifted to the beach on that, for indeed he was lying on planks of wood. Then he remembered the storm and the island and Nausicaa and King Alcinous and the ship full of presents. And he looked for some sign that this small bay was a part of his own little kingdom. The water was full of reflections: a multitude of colors floated there like fruit in a bowl of mulled wine. But there are many such bays in the world.

The bay was guarded by prickly oaks, columnar cypresses, and small, bushy olives. But there are many such trees in the world. He stood up and wandered among the shining presents of King Alcinous, running his disbelieving fingers round the rims of the bronze cauldrons. Perhaps the ship had brought him only as far as Cephalonia or little wooded Zanthe, the outlying islands of his kingdom.

But there! There was the head of Mount Neriton—a shape so familiar to his eye since earliest childhood that it fitted his hopes as a key fits a lock. "I have come home to you, Ithaca," he said. "And when I have cattle and sheep to my name again, I shall sacrifice ten of the finest to Athene, goddess of the gray eyes, who gave me this moment."

He hid the cauldrons, weapons, and other gifts in a cave at the head of the beach, thinking, Home, yes. But safe? For every friend who laughs with joy to see me, a dozen villainous suitors will wish I had died in Troy or on the voyage home. I must take care how I return to Pelicata Palace.

Telemachus, though he sat down at mealtimes with the suitors, spent as little time as he could in their company. Their insults set the blood frothing in his veins, and sweat formed on his brow when he saw how their fingers twitched on their sword hilts at the sight of him. But it pleased him to see the bafflement in their faces. "Who warned you?" said their eyes. "Which god shielded you from harm?" They dared not speak a word of their cowardly ambush.

Caution advised Telemachus not to walk alone in dark places or to stroll along the clifftops when Antinous was close by. When he wanted peace, he went to the hilltop cave where an old pigman tended the king's boars and pigs.

The hungry suitors, with their liking for roast pork, had left the pigman fewer than twenty pigs to tend; he had no need to stray far from his cave and he was always ready to talk to Telemachus about King Odysseus. He was a friend as much as a loyal and devoted servant.

But as Telemachus approached the cave that day he heard scuffling inside, and voices. Cautiously he ducked inside and saw, sitting with his back to the far wall with a fleece pulled round him and over his head, a man who was not the pigman. The stranger looked up, only his eyes showing as he raised food to his mouth. And he looked at Telemachus so piercingly that the boy was half alarmed, half affronted.

"Come in! Come in, my lord Telemachus!" called the pigman from the darker recesses of the cave. "Meet my friend. He's . . . uh . . . he's . . . "

" . . . a shipwrecked soldier," said the stranger. "Crete's my home, and misfortune's been my fate ever since I set sail from Troy."

"Troy? You were at the War?" said Telemachus. "I suppose you saw Odysseus there, fighting alongside Achilles and Nestor and Menelaus?"

"I suppose I did," said the stranger. "And what's he to you?"

"A king, sir, and a hero and a father—and a man who would give you a ship to get you home, if he were able."

"Why, is he poor, then, that he's got no ships in his fleet? I won't believe it! The harbor's full of ships, and that palace up there is not the home of a poor man."

"Oh, but it is," said Telemachus. "It's the home of a man rich in honor but too poor to call one breath of air his own. I'm afraid he's dead, you see. Poor Odysseus is drowned, sir, or pining in some dungeon or sweating over an oar in slavery."

"Then you would be glad, young sir. Surely, a young pike is lord of a pond until the big, old pike comes out from under the weed. You must be glad the old pike is gone."

Telemachus did not hesitate in answering. "Sir, I have no power on this island. I am a ball tossed to and fro between the vermin who have taken over the palace. But if I had all the power of a king and the magic powers of an Immortal, too, I would only use them to wish my father home again, safe and well!"

Odysseus let out a great laugh and threw off the fleece that hid his face and body. Telemachus flinched at the sudden movement, then frowned angrily. "What are you, then? A god from Olympus? You have the look of one, though a god would surely show more kindness than to laugh at the misery of a fatherless son."

Then Odysseus laughed again, at himself this time. "What a fool I am! I thought you'd recognize me, but how could you? I recognize you, of course. Looking at you is like looking into an old mirror where my own reflection has been trapped for twenty years. I'm your father, Telemachus. I am Odysseus!"

Telemachus said nothing. The frown still crouched between his eyebrows, and he turned to the pigman. "He is lying, isn't he?"

"No, lad, he's not lying. This is your own father. I know every feature of his face like I know Neriton Mountain."

"But where's the king's sword? Where's the king's bronze helmet?"

"At the bottom of the sea, along with all my companions and every beam and shackle of the *Odyssey*. But I am not. Finally, boy, that's all I can say—I am neither drowned nor captive. I have come home."

For weeks upon months upon years, Telemachus the prince had smiled and reassured and comforted his mother with brave words. He had been brave—as brave as any full-grown man. Now he laid his forehead on his father's shoulder and wept out loud like a little boy.

As for Odysseus, the hero of Troy, his throat felt as choked as a pipe that the autumn rain pours down and clogs with leaves. He blinked his eyes repeatedly and pulled the fleece forward again over his face.

Telemachus went back to the palace alone for dinner. He seated himself at table with the suitors, ignoring their jibes and the way their fingers twitched on their sword hilts at the sight of him. Queen Penelope sat apart and ate alone in a gallery that overlooked the hall. She ate where there were no knees to nudge her, no eyes to wink at her, no winy mouths to blow her unwelcome kisses.

Out in the yard, the smell of meat reached the ancient hound that lay by the door. Her mangy coat was brindled with gray, her eyes were milky with blindness, and fleas swarmed in her hackles just as the suitors swarmed over the king's property. The dog, who received no kindness from the suitors, sniffed once and twice, but had no hope of a meal, and rested her head back on her paws with a sigh. Then her nose twitched again. A smell reached her that she had not smelled since, as a year-old puppy, she had hunted Ithaca's rocky ravines. Ah, how she had raced then, through the tall grass and scrub, as fast as if her backbone were an arrow fired from her master's bow! She had been happy then, in the days of that smell!

Her ears twitched and her nose sniffed, but all her old eyes could see was a blurred shape against the sunlight. Tremblingly the aged dog rose to her feet on shaking haunches. Her tail began to wag.

"Yes, it's me, Argos, my old companion," said Odysseus under his breath. "But you are the first and last that must recognize me just now." He sat down beside the dog, his back to the doorpost, and Argos laid her old head on her master's lap and died. After twenty years, her long wait was over. She was content.

When the suitors looked up, all they saw was a

ragged and bent old beggar sitting propped in the doorway, nursing a dead dog in his lap. Telemachus called out to the beggar, "Here, old man. You are welcome to come in and ask food from everyone at this table."

The beggar pressed the heel of his hand into his eyes. Then, setting aside the dog's head off his lap, he got up awkwardly and shuffled to the table, with cupped hands, to receive whatever gifts the suitors would give him.

Antinous stole a glance at the queen. "Oh no. Oh no. I couldn't possibly give you anything, you reeking old tomcat. This food belongs to King Odysseus, hero of Troy. We are guests of his wife, the delectable Penelope. What kind of guests would we be if we made free with her food and gave it away to every stinking vagrant who crawled through that door? No, no. I know my duty toward Penelope and the unfortunate Odysseus."

"You mean you want it all for yourself," said the beggar starkly and turned to the next suitor, with his hands outstretched. But Antinous was so furious that he picked up his footstool and hurled it. It struck the beggar between the shoulder blades and knocked him flat, emptying his lungs of air. The other suitors burst out laughing. They threw things, too—bones and plates and boots. Telemachus half rose from his chair, then, as if he had remembered something, meekly sat down again.

It was Penelope who called down from the gallery, "Send the man to me and don't begrudge him a bite of food. My Odysseus may be stranded among strangers. I hope he'd receive kinder treatment at their hands."

She should not have spoken. Her voice drew the eyes of the suitors, and the sight of her put out of their minds all thought of beggars and food. Eurymachus said, "Lady! You have much more important matters to think about. We're waiting. We're waiting to hear your decision. Who's it to be? Who'll sleep in your bed tonight and rule Ithaca ever after?"

"He's right, Mother," said Telemachus, much to the astonishment of Eurymachus. "It is time. I was with the pigman today, and of all the great herds of pig that roamed this island when I was a boy, there are fewer than twenty left. Soon Ithaca will be ruined, and you will be too old to attract a new husband. Unless you want someone to take the crown by force, make a decision and make it now. What Ithaca needs is a warrior strong enough to defend her against her enemies. Set some feat of skill and strength, then rest your fate in the hands of the gods."

All the while he spoke, Telemachus drew nearer and nearer to the gallery, fixing his mother with his eyes and defying her to interrupt him. Her jaw dropped. Her face was ashen white. But Telemachus went on remorselessly, "There! Look, there is Odysseus's hunting bow—the bow he left behind when he took with him his warrior's longbow. Let the man who strings it and fires it into a given target claim my mother and the whole island kingdom of Ithaca!"

Penelope plucked at her skirts, her head ducked forward in grief and confusion and her cheeks flushed red. She searched her mind for the hardest target of all. Then she squared her shoulders and said, "Very well. It shall be as my son advises . . . commands me. You see those axes hanging from the roof? Each one has, at the handle end, a loop for a man's belt to pass through. Set up the axes along the table, handles uppermost. If any man can string Odysseus's bow and shoot an arrow through every loop, let him clutch my hair and call me wife. There. I have said it. And may the gods reward you, Telemachus, for this advice of yours."

Telemachus seemed not to hear. He was collecting up all the shields and swords and spears that belonged to the suitors and giving them into the arms of the servant, Melanthius. When Penelope stayed standing in the gallery watching, her son said, "Very well, Mother. You may go to your room now. I'll tell you when the matter has been decided. Go, and lock the doors behind you."

The suitors were amazed—so amazed that Melanthius had made several trips in and out of the room before any of them noticed him carrying away their weapons.

Eurymachus said, "What's he doing with those?"

Telemachus was quick with his answer. "The smoke from the fire is tarnishing them. I hate to see good weapons ruined. I told Melanthius to polish them all. . . .

Besides . . . I'm afraid, since one of you will undoubtedly win my mother tonight, that the rest of you might start fighting, in your disappointment. That would be a fearful waste of noble blood. You—beggar!—lift down my father's hunting bow, will you? I'm not tall enough to reach it."

But Polybus pushed the beggar aside and snatched the bow off the wall with a loud laugh. "Me first, I think."

He put the bow-tip to the floor and pulled on the other end to bend the bow. But though he heaved and hauled and sweated, he could not bend the bow enough to string it. Another suitor snatched it out of his hands. But he could not bend it either. Eurymachus took the ends of the bow in his two huge hands and tried to arch it. But it was as unbending as the silver spear of the goddess Athene.

"Permit me," said the beggar, taking the bow from Eurymachus.

Bracing it between his right ankle and left hip, he bent the bow and strung it with the yellowing gut that had hung loose for twenty years.

"Give it here," said Antinous, snatching the bow. The axes stood ready by now, their handles upward. He laid one of his own arrows to the bow and took aim along the row of loops. The bowstring hummed. The axes fell like skittles to right and left, and the arrow lodged in the wall.

One by one, the swaggering suitors enraged themselves

with unsuccessful attempts to shoot an arrow through all the loops. Eurymachus, when he failed, hurled down the bow in fury, but when the beggar leaned down to pick it up, he snarled, "Don't even think about it, tomcat. This contest is for the hand of a queen."

"Very well," said the beggar mildly. "I shan't shoot through the loops . . . though in my own country, I've halls and cattle and servants of my own, and I'm better thought of than a beggar by my wife and son."

They turned their backs on him scornfully and called for wine to steady their hands before they began the contest afresh. The beggar gathered up the arrows that had buried their barbs in the furniture and walls. Then he stepped onto a chair and from there onto the table. He drew the bow back to its limit and loosed an arrow. It found its target instantly.

Antinous, who had just raised a goblet of wine to his lips, neither saw nor felt the arrow. As it passed through him, it carried away with it all life and breath and heartbeat. Antinous stood dead on his feet with a look of surprise in his eyes, then fell to the floor, and the spilled wine flowed round his head.

All eyes turned on the beggar. He had thrown off his rags and was naked to the waist, with a heap of their arrows at his feet. His graying golden hair curled across his forehead and deep into the nape of his neck, and the sinews of his arms were plaited like the strands of a great anchor rope.

"Yes, it's my father," said Telemachus, leaping onto the table alongside the stranger. "It is Odysseus. Too late to regret your journeys here to Ithaca, you scum. Too late to call on the gods, you godless vermin. King Odysseus has returned!"

While Odysseus was still traveling, the story of his travels passed from mouth to mouth round the shores of the world-encircled sea. He had come face to face with the terrors of the Known World, and their reflections were in his eyes. When the suitors met his stare, they saw there the Cyclops, the Laestrygonian slaughter, the Scylla, the Sirens, the sea-shifting cyclones, and subterranean spirits beckoning, beckoning them to subterranean shores and endless silence.

Odysseus, the hero of the Known World, was home now, and the world would know of it, come what may!

Chapter Thirteen

The Secret of the King's Bed

THE SILENCE WAS broken by Ctesippus throwing aside the bench that stood between him and Odysseus. He came on with his fists clenched to either side of his body, like a rolling, growling bear, and flung himself forward with such force that Telemachus's spear bent in his hands as he thrust it home into Ctesippus's chest. Then Odysseus's arrows flew. The suitors let out one roar between the fifty of them—a roar as loud as Polyphemus gave as he was plunged into darkness—as they reached for their swords and shields and spears and found they had been tricked.

Melanthius heard the yell—Melanthius the servant, who had played an unwitting part in the downfall of the suitors—Melanthius who had grown rich doing favors for the suitors—Melanthius who had been promised a golden chariot by Eurymachus if he won the queen. "Melanthius! Give us our weapons!" yelled Eurymachus.

Two against fifty; fifty against two. Melanthius thought once, thought twice, grabbed up an armful of swords and spears, and ran to the gallery, from where he flung the weapons down to the suitors below. A dozen were already sprawled facedown, faceup, spiny with arrows.

Telemachus saw the treacherous servant at the gallery rail. "We're betrayed, father!"

Odysseus snorted with contempt. "What? Did the gods preserve my life for twenty years, did they rob Poseidon of his revenge, for a handful of wine-sodden wasters to cut me down in front of my own fire? No! I call on you, Athene, goddess of the gray and furious eyes, to shake your silver spear in the faces of these leeches!"

The size of his voice was enough to strike doubt into the suitors as they struggled with one another for the too-few swords. But when a wind stirred round the roof, and smoke from the fire was forced back down from the ceiling and swirled in choking clouds round them, they were thrown into panic. Like sheep, they panicked—one starting to run and another to follow and two more to follow the leaders. Round and round the table they ran, falling over the dead suitors, falling over the fallers, trampling on live and dead alike. And all the time the bowstring of the royal hunting bow twanged like the bass string of a harp striking the rhythm of a storyteller's poetry.

At the dark end of River Ocean, in the Realm of Shadows, the ancient spirits were jostled by a tumbling-in of strangers. White and ragged strangers somersaulted like acrobats into the halls of the Underworld, with the astonishment of death in their eyes. But no one greeted them. The ancient spirits drifted by without astonishment, nursing their own memories for all Eternity.

"Spare me, Odysseus!" cried a fat and wheezing suitor, throwing himself down at the king's feet and clasping his knees. "I never did any harm! I always told the others that you'd be coming back! Here! Take my sword!"

Odysseus knotted his hand in the man's hair and, looking at his son, asked, "Is it true?"

"He sailed to Asteris with the others to lie in wait for me. And he prayed to Poseidon for your death, while he butchered the finest of your bulls," said Telemachus.

So Odysseus took the fat suitor's sword and cut off his head with one sharp slash.

"Spare me, Odysseus!" cried a thin and hollow-eyed youth, rolling from under the table to clasp the king's feet. "I am only a bard, a storyteller in search of history and truth. I never did you any wrong! Look, I have no sword!"

Odysseus knotted his hand in the lad's hair and, looking at his son, asked, "Is it true?"

"It's true. He's lived on grain gruel rather than eat your beef, and he sang laments when the suitors were too drunk to stop him, and he comforted my mother with stories."

So Odysseus pushed the boy back under the table and, wielding the sword over his head, he leaped down to do battle with Eurymachus, hand to hand.

For weeks, upon months, upon years, Odysseus had suffered at the hands of giants, magicians, the lesser Immortals, and the greatest gods. Now his sword was as murderous as the hands of the Cyclops, the fish spears of the Laestrygonians, the white fists of Poseidon. Eurymachus and every other suitor were hurled name-less into the Realm of Shadows. Only the traitor Melanthius he did not kill in hot blood . . . but afterward, while his blood ran cold with fury.

Silence fell over the dining hall. Even the wind out-side abated, and the smoke rose in a clean column once more, through the roof. The only sound was of Telemachus and Odysseus breathing hard after the vio-lence of the battle.

Telemachus saw his father's eye turn toward the gallery, beyond which Queen Penelope waited. The king went to the foot of the stairs, but halted and turned back and seated himself in a chair by the fire. "You tell her, Telemachus. I've been gone for so long. I can't think what to say. I can't tell how she will feel about me. It's been so many years. . . . "

Telemachus climbed the stairs and knocked on the locked chamber door of Queen Penelope. "You may come out now, Mother. The matter of the suitors is settled."

The door opened a crack, and his mother's face, small and anxious, appeared. "I heard fighting."

Telemachus could not keep from smiling for another

moment. "Yes, Mother! The suitors are all dead! Odysseus killed them. He's come home, Mother! He's come home!" He waited for the laughter to break in her eyes, but she only blinked slowly and her lips narrowed.

"What nonsense is this you're telling me?"

"See for yourself!" cried Telemachus.

Penelope looked over the gallery rail at the figure sitting hunched in thought beside the fire. Telemachus saw her fingers tighten on the rail and her knuckles whiten, but still she did not smile. Sadly and slowly and with queenly poise, she descended the staircase and picked her way between the bodies of the dead suitors. Odysseus rose to greet her.

"Sit down, my lord. You must be weary," she said quietly and seated herself on the other side of the fire, her back erect and her eyes on the flames. Odysseus sank back into his chair. "I shall send a waiting woman to wash your feet and have a bed prepared for you," said Penelope.

Odysseus bit his lip and said timidly, "I would prefer to sleep in my own bed—the bed I carved with my own hands before we were married. It's a thought I clung to while I lay shipwrecked on strange beaches and while monsters ate my companions from round about me and while I lay in my tent below the walls of Troy and while I was washed on a plank of wood across the world-encircled sea."

Penelope slowly nodded her head. "Then I shall have

the bed carried into the great west chamber. You will be comfortable there. I myself will sleep in the eastern-facing chamber. I would prefer it. Is that satisfactory, my lord?"

Telemachus could not believe his ears. "Mother! What is all this? Why are you so cold with him? This is Odysseus! While he was gone your eyes were never dry of tears; not a day passed without you telling us how much you loved Odysseus!"

But Odysseus held up his hand. "Quiet, boy. It must be as your mother chooses. But may I be permitted to ask you one question, Lady?"

"By all means, sir," said Penelope coldly.

"How exactly do you intend to move that bed? I carved it myself out of the crown of an ancient olive tree, and that olive tree grows in the center of Pelicata Palace with its roots still sunk in the Earth and its branches holding up the roof. Forgive my insolence, Lady, but if you can move that bed of mine, I shall cheerfully sleep in the great west chamber or in the pig run or in the yard itself forever and a day."

Then Penelope leaped out of her chair—like a little dapple-coated deer, she leaped over the hearth and into Odysseus's arms, covering his face and hands with kisses.

"Forgive me, my lord! But I was so certain that you were some impostor sent by the gods to break my heart! In twenty years you have hardly changed! I expected a stranger, gray and cruel and covered in scars. I didn't dare to believe that your face could be as lovely as the day you set sail for Troy! Say you forgive me! Say you do!"

Odysseus replied, "My dearest Penelope, if you had not thought up some trick to put me to the test, you would not be a fit wife for Odysseus. The gods made us both quick of hand, but quicker still of wit. And now may I go to bed in the bed of my own making?" And he took Penelope his queen by the hand and led her upstairs to the chamber and to the huge bed of olive wood carved in the crown of a tree.

Sap still flowed in the trunk of the ancient olive, and, here and there, spring leaves were unfolding along the boughs.

After one day, after two days, the feasting and celebrations were over. The dining hall was empty; the house at night lay sunk in sleep; the suitors lay in their graves, more still and silent than sleepers.

Then, at midnight on the third day, out from under the table crawled the thin, young singer of songs whose life Odysseus had spared. He crept out of the palace and down to the harbor. He climbed aboard the smallest of the boats, slipped anchor, and sailed out to sea, ahead of a gentle breeze. Wind and current and rowing carried him, in time, past Cephalonia and little wooded Zanthe, across the open sea, close by a narrow, stony island the shape of a ship, and into the harbor of Scheria. Here, his old blind father sang stories in the court of King Alcinous.

Father and son sat under sunlight and starlight and talked in soft voices, sharing their separate songs.

Their stories they interwove into a new song, and they sang their song at the marriage of Princess Nausicaa. They sang of a king—an ordinary man, not a magician nor one of the Immortals—who had fought under the walls of Troy and whose journeys had taken him from shore to shore of the world-encircled sea. They told how he had escaped death at the hands of monsters, giants, and whirlpools; how he had heard the Sirens' song and been loved by nymphs as lovely as the dawn, with braided golden hair. They told how, finally, he had returned home, to rid his palace of a plague of vermin with the help of his full-grown son.

When they had finished, the bride Nausicaa leaned forward and said, "So, Odysseus's travels are over. Now he can sit under his vines and grow old in the shady places of Pelicata Palace."

"Oh, no, Lady," said the younger bard. "Odysseus has left Ithaca again already, and Penelope sleeps alone in the great olive-wood bed."

"Why?" cried King Alcinous. "In the name of all the gods, where has he gone this time?"

"He's gone with Telemachus, carrying an oar from one of his brightly painted boats. He's set sail for the northern shores of the world-encircled sea, and when he beaches there, he means to travel across the dry land to a place so far from the sea that no sea bird can reach it from any direction—a place where there's no grain of salt in the earth and where no inhabitant has ever heard the name Poseidon. And there he'll plant his brightly painted oar in the saltless earth and make a sacrifice of the finest of his black sheep to the great Earth-Shaker, the Sea-Shifter, the Earthquake-Maker himself. Perhaps then god and man can be at peace again, and the island kingdom of Ithaca will be safe from the vengeance of Poseidon."

The guests at Nausicaa's wedding looked at one another and shook their heads.

"Such a journey!"

"Does such a place exist?"

"How long will he be traveling?"

"Will he ever come back?"

The two bards, father and son, shrugged their shoulders and stroked their hands over their harps to strum small, thoughtful, and harmonious tunes.

Nausicaa got up and stood by the window, looking out at the never-shrinking sea. The waves below her father's palace broke gently against the beetling cliffs and caressed the sharp pinnacles of rock. As one wave arrived, another was always drawing back again, out to sea, out to the open sea that is always traveling, always traveling, always traveling.